BLOOD OF MY BLOOD

Broken Covenant

(Phoebe & Amanda)

First book in The Connected Soul Series

ANDREA JOHNSON

Andrea Johnson Books Publishing

Blood of my Blood – Broken Covenant – Phoebe & Amanda (The Connected Soul Series)

Cover art designed by Andrea Johnson

First published by Andrea Johnson Books Publishing 10/30/20 6565 N. MacArthur Blvd. Suite 225 Irving, TX. 75039 www.AJBPublishing.com

Characters and story based off of the original book: Blood of my Blood, by Andrea Johnson, first published in 2009 © 2009 Andrea Johnson.
All rights reserved.

This is a work of fiction. Names, characters, places and incidents either are a product of the author's imagination, or used fictitiously. Any resemblance to actual persons, living or dead, events or locales, is entirely coincidental.

ISBN- 978-0-578-79454-9

Other Books by Andrea Johnson

The Embryos   **Remember the Promise** **Awaken the Promise**

The King of Credence   **Blood of my Blood**   **The Gates Keeper**

 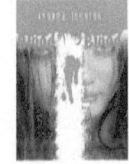 

E-Books

Her Mask   **Vantanka**   **What they don't know**   **Behind the forest**

 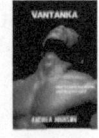  

His Nuclear Requiem   **Voices of Tear Drops**

Andrea Johnson books can be purchased on Amazon.com, or
retail outlets. Or visit Andrea's website at:
www.Andreajohnsonbooks.com

Author's Note

Blood of my Blood was originally released in 2009 as a single book. All four books were included into one novel, and broken down as parts. But I've found that the story delivers a far more greater impact when each character is given their own space.

This story has so many elements to it, that in creating the series, I was able to give the heroes and villains more depth. Adding to their already complex design.

I've made a few changes, implemented a few new twists, and now the series has adapted into something even more intriguing than the single book.

For those of you that may have read the original Blood of my Blood version, you are in for quite a treat.

Because the series is not only something new…the story and characters can only be described as…unexpected. Enjoy.

- Andrea Johnson

BLOOD OF MY BLOOD

Broken Covenant

**Be not deceived. God is not mocked.
Whatsoever a man soweth, so shall he reap.
(Gal. 6: 7)**

PROLOGUE

1978, NORTH CAROLINA

The room was silent as a tomb. She could hear her heart beating inside of her chest like a base drum. The blood pounded in her ears, and the throbbing pain above her eyes had increased. Slowly, the single drop of sweat trickled down the side of her face. Inside of her mouth was a stale metallic taste, the cold undeniable taste of fear.

They were gathered together in the room. All twelve of them. The witches of Melrose. They were impressive, fierce, and they were beautiful. An innocent, harmless group of endearing women surrounded and adored by their people. Or so they appeared to be. In any organization, in many communities, there comes a time when there are those who seek more. Those who seek to control and change. To divide and conquer. There comes a time in any peaceful place, when evil is welcomed in.

Phoebe stared across the room at the others. She tried to remain calm, as her second in command, stood up and walked into the middle of the circle. Every other week, the witches held their meetings in the side room of the community building, that was located at the end of town. The townspeople also used it for holy worship services. Which was one of the reasons, Carolyn, her second in command, had chosen it for their ceremonies. She took sick pleasure in using the sacred place for her sacrilegious purposes.

Phoebe swallowed down the lump of terror in her throat. The coven had not always been twisted and evil. In the recent months since Carolyn had joined them, she'd taken over everything. Encouraging the witches to use their talents for more than healing, and love potions. She had a thirst for power. She craved it, yearned for it. Phoebe knew Carolyn would do anything to uncover the secret that she held deep within her heart. Because she had refused to participate in many of her devious plans for power, they became divided. Six against six. Good against evil. Joining together only for their bi-weekly meetings and plans. In her heart, she knew a change had come to Melrose.

And despite her strength and courage, she feared what she felt. The evil brimming, waiting. And always, watching.

"Tonight, is the night of new beginnings." Carolyn began. She stood in the center of the circle, and slowly stared at each woman as they sat in chairs around her. Her unusual coal black eyes rested a moment longer on Phoebe. Her mouth grinned wickedly.

"My sisters, we must no longer be divided against each other. There is too much at stake. There are lives…at stake."

Her eyes seemed to gleam with a viciousness. Phoebe trembled.

"I would not want any of us to be hurt or disappointed, when unfortunate things suddenly begin to happen."

She turned and locked gazes with her opponent, a sneer on her lips.

"Do you, my dear friend?"

Phoebe hid the stark terror in her heart, at the implied words. She stood to face her. A slight wind blew within the room, and gently ruffled her hair. The beautiful silky white robe she wore, rippled around her willowy body. Her long black hair was like a deep raven blanket that enfolded her. Suddenly, strength and courage emanated from her. Her lovely gray eyes were like storm clouds, moving and erupting, as she stood facing her nemesis.

Carolyn's eyes widened a fraction; at the power, she felt coursing from Phoebe. A sliver of fear took over, and she instinctively took a step back.

"You do not intimidate me, Carolyn." Phoebe spoke softly, but with confidence in her voice. "Me and my sisters are here simply to put a stop to the wrong doings that have taken place in this peaceful town, ever since you arrived. I was mistaken to place you as my second at such an early stage of your training. You are not ready."

Her gaze drifted over to the five ladies who wore white robes identical to hers, then glanced at the others who were draped in black, like Carolyn.

"I've come to tell you that we are all still one. We lived in peace, and love, and joy, and it can be that way again. I only ask that you stop this conspiracy now. There's still time to save yourselves."

"Enough!!"

Carolyn's shout was like a lightning bolt across the sky.

"There will be no saving of anyone, Phoebe! My sisters know of the true power that waits for them. We know of all the riches and pleasures that beg for our discovery, and we know how to acquire it. All of the wonders that you tried to keep from us."

Carolyn raged. Her red hair flamed about her face, like lava erupting from a volcano. Her black eyes were depthless, an eerie and unmistakable clash. She was tall and imposing, her body curvaceous and tempting. Anyone who saw her swore she was a goddess, or the devil's own whore.

"You see, Phoebe my dear, I know about you." She advanced slowly towards her. Like a deadly hungry leopard to its prey. The other women now stood around them, looking on fearfully. She came to within an inch of her. Their noses almost touching. They were of same height, a startling five foot eleven, so they stared each other eye to eye.

"I know your little secret." She whispered. "I know who you are, what you are, and I also know this, sweetheart…"

She inched closer until their lips were slightly touching. The sexual pull Phoebe felt from her, almost brought her to her knees. She fought it, and tried to jerk back, but Carolyn gripped her arms painfully, holding her in place. Her eyes gleamed, as she saw the fear flash across Phoebe's face. She could smell it, and felt the trembling in her body.

"I also know that I will have you. You will be mine. All that you are, and all that you possess." Her tongue slid out and traced Phoebe's lips slowly, seductively. "It will be like taking candy from a baby."

Before Phoebe could react, Carolyn took her face in her hands, and kissed her hard and long on the mouth, in front of everyone. The women gasped in shock and repulsion. She broke the kiss and whispered into Phoebe's startled lips.

"And I'll have your daughter too."

With that, she shoved her to the floor, and began to laugh hysterically. Madness in her eyes. All the women in white, raced towards Phoebe, helping her to her feet.

Dazed and panting in terror at the look on Carolyn's face, she allowed them to lead her out. They held onto her in support as they all quickly filed out of the room. Phoebe shivered. She could still hear Carolyn's wicked laughter even in the warm summer night, as she walked home. But most of all, she remembered her evil promise. It was a constant ringing in her ears.

'I'll have your daughter too.'

CHAPTER ONE

VANESSA DICKENS knelt in the garden and slowly plucked away petals on the roses she held tightly within her hands.

"He loves me, he loves me not." She whispered and giggled to herself as the petals blew away in the soft wind.

"He loves me!" Starry eyed, she lay back in the bed of flowers and stared at the blue sky. There wasn't a cloud in sight. The sky was like a blue ocean, serene and enchanting. A yellow butterfly zigzagged past her face, and she sighed in contentment at the beauty and wonder, that only a young girl in love for the first time, could feel. It had happened so suddenly. She couldn't ever remember not loving, Christopher.

It was only two days ago; Vanessa had gone into town to buy some supplies that her mother needed for the garden. With summer had come the usual chores, and boredom.

She had always been a shy and reserved young woman. Now that she was sixteen years old and her body had gone through some very drastic changes over the past year, she was even more embarrassed about the way the other kids, even the adults, stared at her. The kids in school had never been kind to her. And though Melrose itself was a welcoming place, the school she attended was a few miles outside of their little community. Therefore, the kids were mostly from other larger neighboring towns, and thought of the people in Melrose as freaks. The children often snickered and called her names. Some were bold with their cruelty and would go so far as to threaten to have her and her mother burned on a stake, like in the old days. Vanessa would always run home in tears. She never dared to take the school bus, frightened and embarrassed about who she was. But then her mother, Phoebe, would always brush her tears away and laugh at their foolishness.

"We're no different than doctors." She would tell her, smiling.

"All we do is heal people and tend to their pain. Whether it's emotional, or physical. No one questions a doctor's purpose when that's what they say they are. People automatically know they are there to heal. And so are we."

She was always comforted by these words. Her mom was simply a doctor, she told herself countless times. Everyone in town loved and respected her, and the other ladies in her group. If they chose to call themselves witches, well, it was only the name of their organization. After all, there was no such thing as a real witch.

Vanessa sighed and plucked another rose, remembering. Yes, the last day of school had meant chores, however, she'd looked forward to not having to face her classmates again for a while at least. Until her mom asked her to get some supplies in town. Usually, she wouldn't have a problem going. However, this particular day she'd gotten into a nasty argument with another student, Sandra Rowen. She insulted her mom, and Vanessa had tried to ignore her as she'd been told to do. But Sandra was relentless. When she'd made a comment about Phoebe dancing naked with horns on her head in the moonlight, she could take no more. She hadn't meant to. Really she didn't. But somehow her fist connected to Sandra's face, and sent her flying across the classroom. Vanessa had stood, shaking and shocked to the bone at what she'd done, until Sandra's friends began to chase her home, calling her a witch's daughter. The last thing she wanted was to go into town and see Sandra or her friends waiting to jump her. But her mother insisted. Even after hearing what happened in school.

"It was only a punch," Phoebe laughed it off. "You didn't kill the girl. And she deserved it anyway, but the next time honey, just walk away."
Phoebe kissed her on the nose and hummed silently to herself, while she tended her garden. Vanessa had left grudgingly, prepared for anything. But no one on the face of the earth could have prepared her for what happened next.

She walked into the supply goods store, her list of items in her hand, ready to greet Mrs. Green, the shop owner's wife manning the counter and get the things she needed. That's when she saw him.
He was leaning over the counter and charming the dimples into Mrs. Green's wrinkled face.

"Oh Christopher, you are a devil!" Mrs. Green chuckled and blushed like a school girl.
"You always come in here every Wednesday and try to charm me!"

"Well why shouldn't I charm the most dashing lady in Melrose? There isn't a lady here who can compete with you."

Christopher's voice was deep and husky. It rolled through Vanessa's body like waves crashing into rock. She was dumbstruck. Couldn't move. He was so tall. His hair was a deep curly brown, with different shades streaking through it, like the colors of autumn. His body was a beautiful sculpture of stone and sinew. He was wearing simple gray trousers, which hugged his muscular thighs so tight, Vanessa felt a heat creep through her body as her eyes glanced over them. His white shirt was open at the collar, revealing dark dusky hair on an iron chest.

Suddenly, it was as if he felt her presence.
He turned towards her, and Vanessa's world was never again the same.

Christopher's breath caught at the sight of the vision standing stone still in the door way. The sexual goddess had come to torture him, was all he could think, as he stared.

Her hair was ebony, and it was endless. Long streams of silken black covered her body. Her eyes were like a rich creamy chocolate, sweet and satisfying. And her skin. He felt the drool begin to seep from his watering mouth. It was as smooth as a porcelain doll. Perfect, and untouched. His eyes roamed down the length of her body and rested on her plump and voluptuous creamy breasts. She had on a blue V necked shaped T-shirt and pale blue shorts. Her breasts rose and fell faster, as her breathing quickened while she watched him stare at her.

To Christopher's utter delight, and undeniable torture, he watched as her nipples grew hard as pebbles, and seemed to strain towards him.
The sexual tension inside the store was so thick, you could taste it.

Mrs. Green looked from Vanessa to Christopher, and almost swooned from the side effects. Ashamed, and doubly mortified by her own reaction, she loudly cleared her throat. When that got her nothing, she took a book off of the counter and hit him over the head with it.
"Ouch!!"
"Zip up your pants, you randy bastard!"
Mrs. Green was outraged at his behavior, and secretly jealous. "Don't even think about messing around with Phoebe's daughter. She's not for you. She's the child of a witch."

Christopher saw the pain flash across the beautiful girl's face, at Mrs. Green's cruel words. Embarrassed and humiliated, Vanessa turned and ran out of the store. She tore through town, not seeing anything or anyone. Running all the way to the woods. Her favorite place to think and be alone. Coming to rest by a stream, she plopped onto a log and put her burning face in her hands. She'd never acted like that before in her life. She didn't know what had come over her. Suddenly, there was the sound of running feet. She jumped up and turned. Christopher ran up to her, panting.

"Wait!" He called out, when Vanessa started to run again.

"Wait, don't run away. I won't hurt you. I just wanted to apologize."

He gently took her in his arms and held her closely pressed against him. His breath hitched, as he saw desire heat her eyes. Vanessa was shocked that she felt so comfortable with him.

"I just wanted to know your name." He whispered. Lifting a hand, he stroked a strand of hair away from her cheek.

Vanessa's eyes widened at the feel of his strong fingers on her face. She had never been touched by anyone except her mom and dad.

"Tell me your name, beautiful." He leaned forward to touch her lips, gently, with his own.

"Vanessa." She whispered into his mouth, as their lips made contact. Then they lost all sense of time and place. As he held her, she was kissed for the very first time, and lost her heart to the only man she would ever love.

***

17

Vanessa moaned softly as she remembered the sweet sensuous feeling.

Suddenly, without warning, a dark forbidden eeriness crept over her. Getting up to a sitting position, she looked around. Her senses were alert and filled with tension. It was the weirdest thing. But all of a sudden, she'd felt as if she was being watched.

"There you go imagining things again, Vanessa." She muttered to herself irritably.

"That's what I get for daydreaming when I should be working." Pushing her thoughts of love aside, she knelt in the garden and continued to check for weeds. Humming to herself quietly as she worked, like her mother always did. It was such a lovely day, even for chores. So she'd worn her favorite black shorts and black and white T- shirt, secretly hoping that Christopher would come by. Perhaps she would get to introduce him to her parents. Smiling at the thought, Vanessa worked without a care to the time.

That was how he found her.

Jacob Dickens opened the front door and stood there, watching his lovely daughter. He had been watching her for some time now. Upstairs from his bedroom window. At one point, he thought she had seen him, the way she had jumped up and looked at the house. His little Vanessa. How she'd grown. She was looking more and more like her mother each day.

At the thought of Phoebe, his heart beat faster, and his palms grew sweaty. Some would assume his

reaction was a sign of his desire for his wife. They could not be farther from the truth.
Pasting a smile onto his face, he joined his daughter in the garden.

"Hello, sweetheart." He greeted smoothly, charmingly.

Vanessa's head lifted at the sound of her father's voice. Everything on her beautiful face lit with joy.

"Daddy! I didn't know you were home!"

She dropped her garden tools and leaped up into her father's arms. Laughing joyously, he spun her around.

"I thought I'd surprise you, brown eyes." Her father said gently, calling her by the pet name he'd used since she was a baby.

"Look what I brought for you." He whistled towards the door.

"Oh my God! Daddy you didn't!"

Vanessa nearly wept with joy as a puppy came rushing outside, when he whistled. It was a small golden retriever, so wiggly and full of energy, as she scooped him into her arms.

"I thought mom said I couldn't have one yet."

Jacob's eyes darkened slightly, but Vanessa didn't notice.

"Don't worry about your mom, brown eyes. This is for all your hard work and determination you've shown in school. Besides, aren't you daddy's little girl?"

She beamed with love and adoration up at her father.
"Oh daddy, I love you so much!"
She threw her free arm around her father's waist and pressed her cheek to his solid chest.

Jacob stiffened, and then relaxed as he felt his daughter's arm clasped around him. He looked down at her and tenderly stroked her gorgeous black hair. His heart began to beat faster, and the sweat beaded on his forehead.

Closing his eyes, Jacob willed it away.
But the texture of her hair was so soft. It was a sin to stroke it. My Vanessa, he thought to himself, as he held her close. My little girl. My heart, my joy, my pride, my.....everything.
The burning sensation was starting.
He had to get away.

Vanessa giggled, as the little puppy began to squirm and whimper, trying to move.

"Hey what's wrong little guy? Are you hungry?"
She let go of her father and knelt down to play with her new pet. She didn't see Jacob's stricken expression, his breathing heavy, when she stepped away from him. He shook his head in bewilderment.

"Vanessa..."

Jacob started to reach for her, when he noticed the young man. She saw Christopher at the exact same moment as her father did, and yelped in pleasure and delight.

"Christopher! You came!"

"Of course, I did sweetness."

Christopher held her in his arms as she embraced him. "How could I stay away from the most beautiful girl in Melrose?"

"I thought you had already forgotten me. After all, there are so many more lovely women in Melrose. I'm sure all of them have tried for your attention, Mr. McMann of the McMann Ranch." Vanessa teased him with a playful glint in her eyes.

"Well then they must know that I've only got eyes for one girl. And she's right here." Christopher replied with deep satisfaction.

Vanessa sighed as his lips met hers. He slid his hands down her curvaceous body and skimmed them up the sides of her breasts. Again, they were lost in each other. Oblivious of anything or anyone.
Suddenly, Vanessa's eyes widened, and her cheeks burned in embarrassment, as they broke the kiss.

"Oh my God! Daddy!"

She suddenly remembered her father.

"I'm so sorry Christopher, how stupid of me! I forgot to introduce you to my dad! He's…"

She felt the coldness wash over her, as she turned, only to see her father was already gone. Going into the house quickly, Vanessa looked for him, but he'd vanished. The only thing she saw was the picture frame of the photo of her junior high school graduation.

The one with her smiling in her cap and gown. It sat among three other pictures on the round end table in the hall. A chill swept over her as she slowly walked to the table and picked up the frame. There was just one problem. Her photo was gone. The only thing left, were the pieces of cracked glass sitting within an empty frame.

CHAPTER TWO

Jacob Dickens wore a smile fixed on his face. Anyone who saw him swore he was the happiest man alive. No one ever noticed how the smile was cold and emotionless. Or how dark his eyes were.
Dark and empty.

Jacob worked as the branch manager for the only bank in town. The elegant suits he wore for each day of the week, spoke of his wealth and prestige. He was a tall man. Six foot four, with broad shoulders, and a slim tapered body built like a dancer. Smooth, athletic, and graceful.

His hair was a dirty blond, with streaks of black to the side. He kept it short, and neat. Always slicked back, leaving the impression of a sleek well groomed cat. He only wore crisp stark white shirts. Ironed to perfection, for he would have nothing less.
And his ties always matched his suits.

Jacob sat in his office with his customary smile pasted onto his face; as he listened to a customer speak to him in regards to a loan. His eyes never left his client's face, however, his mind wandered to other things.

His office was immaculate. The cherry wood desk sparkled, the paintings that hung on his wall were of expensive quality.

The chandelier in his office glistened brightly, and the hardwood floor was so shiny, you could stare at your reflection. Idly, he spotted a small piece of lint straying in the air, past his face. Without breaking eye contact with his client, Jacob gently caught the lint with his fingertips and flicked it out the window next to his desk. There would be no lint in his office. No dust. No particles of any kind. Not in his bank, or especially in his house.

Jacob's eyes darkened subtly at the thought of his home, and how he constantly had to clean up after his wife. Oh, she never knew he did, Of course. She must never know. However, his over compulsive disorder seemed to be growing, and it was harder to keep it hidden from Phoebe and Vanessa.

Thinking of Vanessa had the sweat appearing on his forehead again.

Panicked, Jacob fought to remove her from his thoughts. He could not allow the imperfection of sweat to appear on his body. It was unacceptable. But the thought of her remained. The way she laughed, the subtle way her eyes crinkled at the sides when she smiled at him. His heart began to beat faster, and the sweat increased.

He saw Vanessa in her swing as a baby, then he remembered how she looked the other day. When she was unaware he watched her. She'd been taking a shower and thought no one was home. The image of the towel dropping away from that beautiful body of a Goddess, was burned into his memory.

Jacob's body grew hard at the thought, and he willed the feeling away. That's when he remembered seeing her that morning. Embracing that pathetic boy. Throwing herself at him. Giving her love to him. And much more.

This time, the burning sensation sizzled in his chest. Oh yes, he thought to himself. He knew she was giving that boy much more.

"So I really need a loan that will help with the mortgage on the farmhouse, and to bring in much more needed supplies."

The customer was saying to him. Jacob's pasted smile was still in place. No apparent sweat marred his brow, and he spoke efficiently and smoothly to the client.

"What I can do Mr. Stevens, is take a look at your paperwork, and hand it over to my processing department. If everything looks good, we'll give you a call to set up an appointment for an appraisal of your property." His smile appeared like a charming brilliant businessman.

Mr. Stevens was reassured. After all, Mr. Dickens was known in the town for his respectability, honest forthrightness, and dependability. If anyone could get the job done, it was him.

He and his dad had owned the bank for years. His father, Philip Dickens, had started the bank back when Melrose was first built. Now Jacob was the sole owner, and many said he was even more successful at running it than Philip was.

"Thank you, Mr. Dickens, I hope to be hearing from you soon."

He stood up smoothly and firmly took Mr. Stevens' hand, shaking it, then let it go as fast as he could without appearing to be in a hurry to release it. He walked him to the door and quietly closed it behind him.

Immediately, Jacob rushed to the window and closed it down with force. He yanked the blinds all the way down. Panting, he ran to the bathroom, connected to his office, and threw open the medicine cabinet, knocking the bottles down in his haste to find it. He found the bottle of alcohol first. Quickly grabbing a cloth, he poured the alcohol into it and rubbed his hands vigorously, where he'd touched Mr. Stevens, the doorknob, everything.

He had to erase away the imperfections. Hysterically, Jacob rubbed his face, hands, and his arms. Ripping away his shirt and tie, as well as his suit jacket. Jerking off his pants and his underwear until he stood in his bathroom stark naked. Stuffing another cloth into his mouth, so that no one could hear him, he took the bottle of alcohol and emptied it all over his body. He screamed into the cloth, as the liquid made contact with the nicks and gashes that were all over him. He splashed it especially on his groin area, thinking of Vanessa. "I will not fail!!" He shouted. "I am perfect! I am perfect! I-AM-PERFECT!!!"

***

Jacob stared at himself in the mirror. All traces of evidence were gone. The bathroom was again immaculate. Every bottle back in its place. The mirror scrubbed to an impossible shine. The floor was dry, and sparkled with cleanliness. His clothes had been disposed of. Placed in a small brown box to be taken out to the end of town and dumped deep in the woods. There, it would be buried. Right along with all the other boxes he had buried there each week. He'd already replaced his suit. A fine silk black, with matching tie.

No one would ever notice the difference, for it was the exact replica of the former one he'd been wearing. Jacob carried a wardrobe of six pairs of identical suits each week to work, inside a box in the trunk of his car, at the crack of dawn each day. No one was ever the wiser.

Staring at himself in the mirror, his face was bland. A granite picture of coldness. Slicking his hair into place, he opened the medicine cabinet, and found it.

Opening the bottle, he tipped back his head and drank greedily. Sighing in contentment, he covered the bottle and replaced it in the cabinet. He looked at himself once again in the mirror and pasted the smile back on his face.

"Back to work as usual, Jacob." He said quietly, grinning at his reflection.

CHAPTER THREE

"I don't know why you put up with it, Phoebe."

The woman stared at her from across the room and spoke in silent hushed whispers. Phoebe smiled indulgently, for she knew what was coming.

A long unavoidable lecture which her best friend, Amanda, had been waiting all week to give her. She sighed and began to pack away her bottles of medicines and spell potions into her small bag she carried with her, each time she met with a patient. Phoebe knew the subject could not be avoided for long. She'd been putting off Amanda's lecture for over a week now. Ever since that frightful last meeting the witches had together. She shivered involuntarily as she remembered it, and stubbornly pushed the thought aside.

Right now, she was at work, and though she knew they had to talk about what must be done, she'd rather not discuss it in a patient's home.

"Amanda, I know we need to talk about the different things that have been going on. But right now, I have other patients I need to see, and I don't want to discuss personal business in their homes." Phoebe said dismissively.

Amanda snorted rudely.

"Don't give me that nonsense, Phoebe!"

She stood and crossed the room to face her. She was breathtaking. Her long wavy, auburn colored hair hung down her back. Swishing around her as she walked. In her anger, her lovely green eyes seemed to glitter like emeralds. Her sensuous mouth was drawn into a frown, set in an exotic looking heart shaped face. Her body was unbelievable. Toned and curvaceous. She was also tall and willowy like Phoebe. But as Phoebe was gentle and softhearted, Amanda tended to be direct and outspoken. She was definitely the bolder of the two.

Amanda stood with her hands on her hips, clad in tight jeans and shirt, angrily staring at her best friend.

"This is not a matter you can just dismiss and discuss later over a cup of tea! Your very life is in danger!" Amanda's voice had risen in her anger. Phoebe's eyes sparked that same fury, as she draped her bag over her shoulder and turned to her.

"I will not have you raising your voice and shouting inside of Mrs. Holloway's home!" She hissed at her. Her Voice was like a slap.
"She is a very sick woman, and I will not have you upsetting her. We will deal with this later."

"When will later be, Phoebe?" Amanda grabbed her arm in desperation. "When you're dead? When there is nothing more anyone can do because it's too late?"

Phoebe started to retort, then she saw the expression in Amanda's eyes. There was fear there, hurt, and most of all pain. Pain for her.
Startled, Phoebe took her hands in her own.

"Don't fear for me, dear sister. All will be well. I know you worry about me and little Vanessa, but we'll be okay. After all, we have Jacob to take care of us."

With that, she embraced her and held her gently. As they left Mrs. Holloway's house, Phoebe was oblivious to the tremor that swept over Amanda's body. The thought of Jacob taking care of them, was exactly what she feared most.

***

During Phoebe's daily visits to her patients' home, she always had Amanda accompany her. She worked as her assistant and was very efficient at her job. Wherever you saw Phoebe, there was Amanda.
They were two of the most loved, and well known, among the witches in Melrose. Some say they were actual sisters, as they seemed to always be inseparable. At least, until Phoebe had married and started a family of her own.

Amanda had always been against the marriage. But many thought it was due to jealousy, at no longer having her best friend around all the time. If they only knew the truth.

Phoebe smiled contentedly, as they walked side by side down the main street in town.
Not many cars drove by. The people who walked along the sidewalks would wave at them or smile in greeting. Occasionally, she would see a fellow witch, on her way to a patient. Melrose was not big, but it was prosperous.

She looked proudly at the bank her husband owned. The milliner's shop. The supply goods store, where Mr. and Mrs. Green held tight reins. The grocery store, where old Mrs. Basely kept all of their food products. The bakery, where Mr. and Mrs. Fisher had recently become the new owners. They were expecting their first child any day now.

Bethany Simpson, who was also a witch, was the one assigned to the care and handling of the birth. Phoebe smiled to herself at the thought.
Bethany was so nervous. It was going to be her very first delivery, and she'd asked her to be there. She had consented, but Phoebe knew she would do fine. Bethany was a beautiful, capable, and reliable young witch. She was confident in her capabilities.

Stopping at the supply goods store, she and Amanda went inside and greeted Mr. Green, standing at the counter writing up inventories. He was a small, balding man, with a huge smile.

"Well hello Phoebe, Amanda." Mr. Green welcomed them, his mouth spreading in a wide grin. "Now I don't even need any sunshine, you two have just brightened my day!"

Phoebe laughed, delighted. The sound was like a warm summer breeze. Amanda grinned and hugged Mr. Green affectionately.

"It's good to see you John. How are Rosy and the grand kids?" Amanda engaged Mr. Green in a conversation about him and his elderly wife, and their four grown kids, and grandkids who had moved away.

Phoebe began to browse the store. Looking for the supplies that Vanessa had not picked up, only two days ago, she frowned as she remembered.
She wouldn't explain to her what happened in town. She knew she'd had a problem in school, but Phoebe didn't think that was what had made Vanessa dash through the house, her cheeks blushed red and her hair windblown. Her frown deepened.

Her daughter had not been as open about her feelings lately. It didn't help matters at all, when she'd come home earlier today for lunch, and discovered that Jacob had bought a puppy for her.
Phoebe moved along the aisles, bothered by her thoughts.

He hadn't even discussed it with her. She thought sadly. She wanted to give Vanessa a puppy for the fourth of July. It was supposed to be a surprise. She had talked it over with him, but he'd discouraged it. Insisting that Vanessa told him she didn't want a puppy.

When Phoebe got home earlier and saw the absolute joy on her daughter's face as she held the puppy, her heart felt as if it had been stabbed.

"Look what dad brought me, mom!" Vanessa gushed at her. Phoebe had smiled, congratulating her on the present. Making it seem like she had known all along. She called Jacob right away and asked him about it.

"Why didn't you tell me you were going to get it for her?" The hurt was plain in her voice.

"Oh, I'm so sorry, honey." Jacob said smoothly. "It was all so sudden. She had decided that she wanted a puppy after all, and I didn't want to waste any time. You understand, don't you sweetie?"

His charming seductive voice had melted her doubts. Now, however, she wondered if she was missing something. The old familiar fear rose up inside of her. She reminded herself to corner Vanessa and try to get to the bottom of things.

Purchasing her supplies, she and Amanda left the store and started back to Phoebe's house.
With patients tended to for the day, and the shopping done, Amanda felt that now was as good a time as any, to begin their talk. They walked quietly along the road.

"She's out of control, Phoebe. It's not just a small problem anymore, like we had first thought when she

34

arrived in Melrose." Phoebe stayed silent as Amanda spoke to her.

"I told you it was a mistake to include her into the coven. Especially when you made her second in command! From the first time I saw her I noticed how she looked at you, with this gleam in her eyes."

Amanda shook her head.

"Black eyes with red hair? Naturally born? It's unheard of, Phoebe. She smelled like trouble, but you wouldn't listen. You wanted to give her a chance, wanted the town to accept her. Knowing they would, automatically, if you made her one of us."

"She has a special gift for healing." Phoebe argued.

"It's not a gift, but a curse she has! And she doesn't use it for healing. You know this as well as I do." Amanda replied angrily.

"Anyone can change, Amanda."

"You wanted to reform her!!" Amanda shouted back, losing control on her patience.
"You saw the evil in her, bibi, and you ignored it! You convinced us love would change her. Make her better. You pushed our worries aside, and now, look at what has happened!"

Amanda fought back her tears of frustration, as she raged at her. She tried to calm herself.

"She has divided the coven. We are no longer one. Six against six. Good against evil, and more are slipping into her control each day!"

The tears that began to fall down Phoebe's cheeks were dashed aside, as she listened to Amanda's pain and fear.

"Things will get better." She said stubbornly.
"The power is still ours. She cannot possess what we have."

"Phoebe, don't you understand?!" Amanda grabbed a hold of her arms and jerked her to face her. "Carolyn already knows."

Coldness gripped her heart, as Phoebe's eyes widened in fear. She stared into Amanda's grief stricken gaze. "No." She whispered. "That can't be true. It's not possible."

"Remember what happened at the last meeting. I heard what she said to you. I saw what she did. I saw the knowledge of it in her eyes!" Amanda shouted.

Phoebe jerked away in terror.

"Stop it!!" She shouted in denial, backing away. Her face was pale.

"You know it's true." Amanda said softly. "You see the truth every day, Phoebe. You must put a stop to it, before it's too late." Her face was wet with tears, as she reached for her friend.

"She knows our secret."

Amanda could hold it back no longer, as she said the words Phoebe had never wanted to hear.

"And so does your husband."

Phoebe held the scream inside. Not wanting to give into the pain. Refusing to listen to anymore, She left Amanda standing on the side of the road, her tears, like an echo of the beginning of the end.

CHAPTER FOUR

Sarah Davidson prided herself on being smart. She grew up in a family of ten brothers and sisters, and almost always had to fight for what she wanted. She had to scream in order to be heard over all the other voices and demands of her siblings. Ambition was rooted deep within her. Without it, she'd still be simply child number eight, with a number and an ID tag, hung around her neck. Her mother had slept with so many men, she didn't know what child came from whom, or on most occasions, even remember what the child's name was. So her mother had made them all ID tags.

One time she even threatened that if they didn't wear them, or God forbid lose them, they would not be allowed in the house, or given any food.
Many times, it took the police knocking on the door, in order for her mother to relent.

Sarah had been determined from the tender age of ten that she would rise above the filth of the life she had with her family. If it could be called that. She had prostituted, stole, ran every kind of scam she could think of, in order to save up and get out of New Jersey. She'd hooked up with a gambler who had been heading to Las Vegas and had offered to take her along with him.

Sarah had known better than to trust anyone. Although she'd still gone along in hopes of winning it big in Vegas or landing a great opportunity.

It was not to be.

The man, he called himself Snake, had pulled over on the side of the road after they had been traveling for about ten hours.

He'd taken Sarah by surprise, and dragged her out of the car, pulling her into nearby woods. He'd raped her. No matter how much she'd fought, she'd still lost the battle. He'd taken everything she had saved within the last ten years of her life, and he'd left her there. Broken, bleeding, and half conscious.

Sarah parked her car in front of the small brown house and brooded silently on the past. Her short curly blond hair blew around her face. Her eyes were a cold sea blue. Her pale face lacked all softness, which gave it a hard, 'fuck the world' sort of look. Her body was in great shape. Toned and firm with muscle. She was slim, tall and curvy. Her body was what had always gotten her by, not her brains. However, this time was different.

Sarah got out of her car and slammed the door. Staring at the house, a slow devilish smile began to spread across her hard face. Now, her brains and slick ways were all that was needed here. Sarah knew all she'd had to do was give it time. Be patient. Play along. Act the role of the innocent lost victim, until the next opportunity came along. And it had.

Its name was Carolyn Lee O'Neil.

She walked up to the house with anticipation and excitement. The place was old and worn. The windows needed cleaning, and some were slightly cracked. It was a two story cottage nestled a little outside of town, deep within the woods. The grass was overgrown. It gave the house a long abandoned look. Its ugly brown color only added to the effect.

Walking through the grass, Sarah stepped up onto the cracked broken porch, and knocked loudly on the screen door. Carolyn had only moved into the house two months ago, and she knew the place suited her well.

After a moment, the door was opened. She smiled in greeting as Kathryn, a member of the coven, let her into the house.

"You're late, sister Sarah."

Kathryn sneered at her, as she sauntered through the door. Sarah simply smiled and blew her a kiss. She walked down a short hallway, noting the dust that covered the walls, and the thin brown carpet that was tracked with dirt.

Carolyn was not interested in housekeeping.

As she entered a large room, being used as the living area, Sarah was not surprised to see everyone already

40

seated and waiting for her. All three witches sat comfortably watching her, as she entered.

Roselyn Jackson sat in the loveseat, surveying her with her dark, mysterious brown eyes. Her curly brown hair was pulled back into a ponytail. She was the shortest one of the group. Petite and dainty. Today she wore a white cotton dress that rose above the knees when she sat. She was also the quietest. Sarah was always watching her.

Directly across from Roselyn, sitting on the sofa, was Amy. No one knew too much about her. She was of average height, with plain straight brown hair, and was skinny as a toothpick. Everything about Amy was plain and boring. She wore glasses that were constantly slipping off her nose, and always wore plain black slacks, and a buttoned down white blouse. Her driving motivation had always been to be beautiful. To be like everyone else. She would do anything to obtain it.

Coming in to join them, sitting down at the other end of the sofa, was Kathryn Rogers. The one who had opened the door for her.

Kathryn was the woman you loved to hate. Her body was perfect. All legs and curves tucked snugly in a tight black top and matching mini skirt that left nothing to the imagination. Her firm breasts were always the center of attention. But above all, there was one thing Sarah hated her most for. The one thing that had made her Carolyn's number one assistant.

41

Her long wavy black hair. It was not silky smooth and flowing like Phoebe's. However, just the color and length of it, had a great likeness to her. And for that reason alone, was why Kathryn was treated better than anyone else in Carolyn's circle. They all knew how much Carolyn coveted Phoebe.

Sarah's blood boiled, as Kathryn took her place directly next to Carolyn, on the sofa.
As she settled, she smiled knowingly at her. Sarah vowed silently to herself that it would not be that way for long. Pulling up a chair she sat down, and patiently waited for their leader to begin. Carolyn rose and walked to the front of the room.

The area was large enough to hold more furniture, however, only the sofa, loveseat and a few chairs remained. A small wooden coffee table sat in the middle. The rest of the room was barren. There was no other furniture in the house, except for the upstairs master bedroom, where Carolyn slept.
She did not require much for what she intended to do. Only time. Time, and patience. Now, both were on her side.

"We have waited long and planned very hard for this day." Carolyn turned and faced the members of her group.

"We cannot afford for anyone to have second thoughts, or second chances."

She looked at Sarah, a small smile appearing on her red lips. "There will be no other opportunity for what we seek. Are there any questions?"

Roselyn slowly raised her hand, her heart thudding in her chest.

"Yes, Roselyn?" Carolyn's voice was crisp with impatience.

Roselyn visibly swallowed.

"Is this the only way to receive the power? I mean, do we have to do this to Phoebe?"

Her question was met with a deadly silence. Sarah mentally shook her head. Roselyn, you should've stayed quiet. She thought to herself.

"Don't you want what the power can do for you, Roselyn?" Carolyn asked, slowly advancing on her. There was a feral glint in her eyes that warned her that she had made a fatal mistake. Roselyn knew she was in danger.

"Y—yes of course!" She tried to laugh it off. "Of course I do, Carolyn! I was just wondering why we have to go through all of this to get it."

Roselyn's chin went up a fraction as she boldly stared at her. Carolyn began to chuckle. How nice. She thought to herself. To be so brave, yet so foolish.

"Do not worry, sweet Roselyn." Carolyn said soothingly. "Everything is quite under control."

***

The meeting was over, and Amy and Roselyn had already left to go home. Only Kathryn and Sarah remained with Carolyn.

"You know what we have to do about her, don't you?" Said Kathryn. She was sprawled out on her stomach on the sofa. Her long legs swinging back and forth. She knew she made an erotic picture, with the bottom of her skirt riding up past her buttocks, and her hair falling around her oval face.

Sarah crossed her legs and leaned back in the chair. "You wouldn't even know how to do it, idiot. That has to be left to me."

"Enough!" Carolyn shouted at both of them. "Kathryn is right. Roselyn is a loose end. She needs to be snipped, before she destroys everything we've planned."

Sarah stood up and walked over to her.

"Leave it to me, Carolyn. Let me handle her. I've never trusted her from the beginning."

Carolyn watched the hungry gleam in Sarah's eyes, and smiled in satisfaction.

"Yes," she whispered, lifting a hand and stroking her cheek. "I think you would do the job very well."

Sarah smiled and purred low in her throat, like a cat being stroked by its master.

CHAPTER FIVE

Roselyn did not go straight home after the meeting. Perhaps it was instinct. Maybe it was fear. All she knew was that she could not go home right now.

Darkness had fallen, and most people were in bed. Hurrying down the empty street, she made a last minute decision to go to her best friend's house. Bethany Simpson.

Bethany still belonged to Phoebe's group. She had tried to convince Roselyn to stay with her.

"There's something strange about her, Rossi." Bethany had said to her one day, after seeing to a patient. "I don't know, but she seems distant, almost....evil." Roselyn had laughed off her fears and told her that she didn't know how to live life dangerously.

"She's completely harmless!" Roselyn insisted. "All she wants to do is liven things up a bit. Dabble in a little real magic."

As Roselyn raced past the stores on main street, she could only wish she had listened to her friend. She and Bethany had been friends with Phoebe ever since they had moved to Melrose. They almost all grew up together.

When Phoebe had started the coven, it had seemed like a wonderful idea. Helping people and having everyone look at you like you were someone special. Roselyn had forgotten all about that. The joy. The beauty. It had made her so much more than she was. An average woman, with average ambitions. To get married and have kids. Now, with sadness, Roselyn realized she'd gotten mixed up into something dark and sinister. And with a sinking feeling, she knew she wasn't going to be coming out. Alive.

Running harder, the tears streaming down her face, she reached her friend's house and banged loudly on the door.

"Bethany!!" She shouted, taking quick glances behind her. She could feel someone watching her. "Bethany please! Open the door!!" Roselyn heard movement behind her. She turned quickly, but there was no one there. Just then the door opened, and Bethany's husband, Derek, stood there with a shocked expression on his face.

"Roselyn is that you? Are you alright?" He asked her, Opening the door wider to let her in.
He took in her tears and the violent shaking, and immediately led her to the couch in the living room.

"Just hold on a second, I'll get Bethany."

Not wasting a second, Derek raced up the stairs and ran into the master bedroom. He hurried to his wife's sleeping form.

"Beth, wake up! Roselyn's downstairs, she needs you."

Bethany instantly became alert at the urgency in her husband's voice.

"What happened? What's wrong with Rossi?" She didn't wait for an answer. Slipping into a robe, she hurried down the stairs. Her short cut brown hair was gently tousled from sleep. Her lovely brown eyes widened, as she took in her friend's condition. Roselyn's white dress clung to her body with sweat. Her face was ravaged from crying, and her eyes were red and filled with terror.

"Rossi!" Bethany ran and enfolded her in her arms. Roselyn wept even harder, at her friend's embrace. Bethany signaled her husband to go put on a pot of tea.

"Sweetie what happened?" She asked her gently. "Are you hurt? Please tell me."

Bethany tried to calm her by rocking her back and forth. Finally, Roselyn began to settle down, her sobs turning to low hiccups. She took the tissue her friend offered and tried to compose herself.

"I should've listened to you, Beth." She hiccupped. "You were right all along. But it's a lot worse than any of us thought!"

"Okay, take it easy. I want you to start from the top. What happened?"

Roselyn took a deep breath and told her everything. By the time she was finished, Bethany's blood was cold, her eyes were wide with fear and terror.

"We have to stop her!" Roselyn pleaded with her, grabbing her hands. "She's out of her mind! She's going to kill her!"

Bethany stood abruptly and began to pace the room. Her slim athletic body was taut with tension. Her beautiful face marred with fear and despair for the friend she loved.

"I've seen it." She whispered, turning to Roselyn, her body trembling. "I've been having these nightmares lately, now every night. About a dark place. And there's screaming, and blood. So much blood everywhere."

She put her face in her hands to chase away the images from her mind.

"We have to stop them, Beth." Roselyn rose from the couch and went to her, lightly touching her shoulder. "We can't let them do this to Phoebe."

As Derek came in with the cups of tea, they all sat down again, trying to figure out what to do.

"We have to tell her." Bethany stated.

"She won't listen." Bethany replied flatly. "The only one she might listen to, regarding this, is

Amanda. You know how Phoebe gets anytime we discuss Carolyn." She sighed. She doesn't want to believe that she's capable of something like this."

Derek shook his head, his face grave.
"Then someone needs to make her listen." He said.

"Amanda will." Bethany held a look of determination in her eyes. "She'll make her listen."

***

After Roselyn had gotten herself under control, she insisted on going home.

"But you can't!" Bethany pleaded with her. "What if they find out you've told me?!"

"Trust me." Roselyn said, kissing her friend's cheek for what she knew was the last time.
"They already know. If I stay here, I'll put you and your family in danger."

She cut her off when Bethany tried to argue.
"You have children, Beth." She whispered, her eyes watering. "Take care of them."

It was the only thing that made her back down, as Roselyn had known it would.

Now, as she walked the dark streets, she knew she was being followed. It would make no difference where she ran, they'd still come after her.

Suddenly, Roselyn decided to change directions. Heading instead, towards the woods. What better place to die than the place she had lived and loved for most of her life? She did not run. Even when she heard the footsteps following her into the woods.

The trees seemed to close around her. Enclosing her inside of the darkness. Like a coffin.
She stopped on a hill that during the day, if you climbed the tree growing tall above it, you could see the whole town.

Funny the things you treasure when you know you're about to die.

"I never trusted you." Sarah's voice cut through the quiet. "I always knew you would betray us."

Roselyn turned to face her.

She was leaning nonchalantly against a tree. Her arms crossed. A gun dangling in her left hand.

"You know, I could kill you right now if I wanted to. But what fun would there be in that?"

Sarah chuckled.

"Oh yes." She put the safety on the gun.
"First, I'm going to have a little entertainment."

She advanced on her.

The moon was high in the sky. The townspeople deep in slumber. Too deep to hear a woman's screams of torture.

CHAPTER SIX

Christopher McMann galloped through the fields on his black stallion, Dominance.

The wind sang in his curly brown hair, as he shouted up at the sky. He'd never felt more on top of the world than he had, these past two weeks. He was in love, and he wanted it to last forever. Just twenty one years old, he had to wait at least another three years before he could receive his inheritance and take over the ranch. But he would ask her tonight.
He would ask Vanessa Dickens to be his wife.

Christopher galloped faster, as he thought of holding her in his arms again. Her lovely smile, her soft beautiful body. He would make her his, tonight. Tonight, they would make love for the first time, and then he'd ask her. They would be secretly engaged until his inheritance, because he knew his father would never approve. He had yet to formally meet her parents, but from what he had glanced of her father that day, he didn't think they would approve either.

Pushing these thoughts aside, Christopher Slowed Dominance to a trot as he approached her.
She was standing in a field of violets. Her hair left loose to flow around her shoulders, just as he liked it. She had a violet stuck in the side of her hair that made her look like a Hawaiian girl. Today, she wore a

blue summer dress. The skirt billowed around her legs in the breeze, making his mouth water.

He reigned Dominance and tied him to a nearby tree.

"I've been waiting for you." Vanessa said softly, as he gently took her in his arms.

"Now I'm here, beautiful. I'm not going anywhere."

Her arms came around him, as their lips met in contentment. Vanessa felt her body soar, as Christopher's hands began to stroke her face, her hair, then glided slowly down her body.

"Vanessa, my love, I need you."

He began to rain sweet kisses over her face. Kissing her eyes, her nose, her cheeks, and then returned back to her mouth. She moaned deep in her throat, aching with love for him. It was almost painful. She had never felt this way before, and it scared her. Slowly, he lowered her into the bed of flowers. They were surrounded by their sweet perfume. He kissed her neck, tenderly grazing his tongue over the pulse that throbbed there.

Vanessa jerked in amazement at the thrill that raced through her body. Taking his time, Christopher lowered the strap of her dress, and bared a smooth creamy shoulder. He rained it with kisses, gently following it to her plump cleavage.

She arched her back, as a spark of pleasure shot through her. Slowly, he traced the soft round curve of her breast with his tongue. Craving her, needing her. Vanessa moaned. She was assaulted with all of the delightful feelings he was bringing to her. She wasn't quite sure what it was she wanted, but she knew she needed it now.

Christopher watched the emotions flash across her beautiful face and had to fight for control. Slowly, he lowered her dress down to her waist, and bared her lovely round breasts for his greedy view and pleasure. Tenderly he captured a nipple within his teeth and began to suckle it. Tasting her. Starving like a newborn babe. She cried out in shock, as the first wave rushed through her body. She arched and threw back her head, moaning as the spasms wracked her. Holding her, Christopher's hands slowly stripped the dress off of her completely, her thin dainty panties following along in its wake.

Vanessa's legs trembled, as her bare skin made contact with his mouth.

"Christopher," she sobbed, "please."

She didn't know what she asked for; she only knew that he was the only one who could answer her every need. But Christopher continued in his slow torture. Slowly nipping the skin beneath her breasts, making his way down her torso. Vanessa was panting, the sweat beaded down her body, as she fought to control her emotions. But it was impossible.

55

The things he was doing to her was incredible.

Taking his tongue, Christopher slowly dipped it inside of her very enticing belly button. She cried out his name, her body pulsing with sweat and desire. She reached for him, wanting to touch him. But he resisted her hands, continuing in his slow appreciation of her delectable body. Reaching her curly mound, he tenderly parted her soft flesh, and placed his lips deep within her. Vanessa cried out in pleasure and agony, as the climax ripped through her body, wrenching her very soul. The tears fell from her eyes as she sobbed his name, begging him to come to her.

Christopher could hold back no longer. He threw off his clothes and rose up to meet her.

"Sweet Vanessa."

He took her face in his hands and kissed away her tears.

"Let me show you how much I love you. How much I need you."

Taking both of her hands, he raised them above her head and held them firmly pinned to the ground, as he entered her in one hard thrust.

Vanessa's body jerked at the instant of pain that slashed through her. Her eyes widened in shock. But as he began to move within her, the feeling of elation returned. She began to float again, this time higher, farther than she'd been before, because now he was with her.

"Vanessa…."

Christopher rasped out her name, as her flesh tightened around him. Enclosing him like a warm glove, feverishly driving him to the point of no return. He watched, as her eyes widened in confusion and began to water, as she was hit with a violent orgasm. Her body bucked and arched, as she rode the delicious pleasure coursing through her. Christopher felt the tremors of her flesh and was lost. Together, they submerged head long into the endless abyss of love.

***

Lying naked in the flowers, Vanessa sighed contentedly as she lay nestled within the comfort of her lover's arms.

"I wish we never had to leave here. I wish this moment would last forever." She said, gently kissing the arm that was wrapped securely around her.

As Christopher kissed the top of her silky head, he suddenly got a feeling of dread at Vanessa's innocently spoken words. A premonition of terror and despair. She felt the stiffness in his body and turned to stare up at him.

There was a weird look in his eyes.

"Baby, what's wrong? Is everything okay?" She touched his cheek in concern. The touch of her hand brought him back with a jolt, and he jumped, startled.

"Christopher, what's the matter?!" Vanessa cried out, as he jumped away from her, staring at her with a funny expression on his face.

His eyes had the look of a frightened deer. He couldn't explain it to her. How her words had triggered a dark vision. A vision of her screaming in pain and terror, and the blood that was everywhere, and the...the......

"Christopher, you're scaring me! Please tell me what's wrong!" Vanessa pleaded with him. She stood before him, oblivious to her nakedness. Looking like a wood sprite in her beauty. Slowly, he regained control of his emotions, and shook the image of death from his mind.

"I'm sorry," he apologized, taking her in his arms and kissing her. "I don't know what came over me. Let me take you home."

As they prepared to go, thoughts of marriage proposals were the furthest thing from his mind.

CHAPTER SEVEN

Phoebe entered her home and dropped her bag on an end table in the hallway. She sighed and rolled her aching shoulders, as she entered the living room. As usual, it was immaculate. Jacob had a thing for cleanliness.

Oh, he'd tried to hide it from her, but she knew he loved everything in order. So she tried her hardest to please him. Thinking of Jacob, a small frown creased her lovely brow, as she remembered what her best friend had said to her only a few weeks ago.

"He knows." Amanda had whispered, her voice trembling. A trickle of fear began to spread through her chest as she sat down at her office desk, situated in the corner of the living room.

It couldn't be true. Phoebe thought to herself, as she began to unpin her hair from its tight bun. Gently, she started to massage her tense scalp. It suddenly dawned on her that Jacob was always the one who used to do that. Now, he never even touched her anymore. Almost everything about him had changed, since she married him, seventeen years ago. The over compulsiveness, the strange distant attitude he displayed towards her. The.... secretive and sudden midnight disappearances he'd been having as of late. Especially his reaction whenever he was around Vanessa. Her heart quickened. What was going on? Was Amanda right all along? Had her marriage been a mistake?

Phoebe's heart began to ache, as she remembered a long ago love. A rare and indescribable thing that she had held and lost. She had promised herself to never look back. That was all in the past. She was married to Jacob now and he was a wonderful husband.

Shrugging it off, she dismissed her suspicions as foolishness, and blamed Amanda for putting them in her head. Thinking of Amanda brought her mind to the previous day's events.

A search party had been issued for Roselyn Jackson. She had been missing for almost two weeks now. The frown deepened on her forehead, and the worry returned. Along with it, came the fear she tried so hard to keep at bay.

After several days of searching with no success, Amanda had told Phoebe that she'd spoken with Bethany. Roselyn's closest friend. The fear increased as she remembered all that she had told her.

"She knows Carolyn's behind it." Amanda had said to her. "Even though the state police questioned her and found no evidence at either her or her group member's homes, Bethany knows Carolyn is somehow responsible for Roselyn's disappearance. And she's afraid she might be next. Phoebe, when will you wake up?!!"

Phoebe sighed and rose from the desk, heading upstairs. She and Amanda had a big fight over it yesterday.

"I'm tired of hearing about you trying to protect me!"

Phoebe had shouted back at her.

"In case you haven't noticed, I'm a thirty six year old grown woman! I am well capable of protecting my own life, now stay out of it!!"

The sadness welled up in her, as she remembered stomping away from Amanda. She'd walked away from her best friend, who was so much more to her than anything else in the world. So much more. She was a part of her. More than anyone could know. And Phoebe was determined that no one ever would. Going into the bathroom, she stripped off her clothes and let the cool shower wipe away all of her fears.

***

Jacob watched her as she lathered herself with soap. The bubbly water trickling down her smooth curvaceous body. He watched her with a calculating eye. His jaw clenched tightly in anger. She simply didn't care about the mess she made when she came into the house. The splashes of water all over the bathroom floor. His blood boiled, as he tried to bring himself under control. But it was getting harder.

Jacob's hands clenched into fists, as he watched his beautiful wife, carelessly humming a tune as she showered. As if she didn't have a care in the world. His tongue slowly began to trace his lips in anticipation.

The time was almost right. When his beautiful witch of a wife would pay dearly for her sins. All of the years of waiting, of planning, would finally pay off. His eyes glazed slightly, as he imagined her sexy body in his hands. Torn, broken, and completely at his mercy. But he had to bide his time. He sneered, as he slowly backed out of the bathroom.

The brightness that was always present around Phoebe blocked him from coming any further. He couldn't even touch her anymore. Her spirit saw the darkness in his, even if she herself was blind to it.

As he backed away, he saw the puppy he had given to Vanessa, cowering in the hallway. Its little body shaking in fear as it whimpered and scampered away from him down the hall. Blissfully unaware of his presence, Phoebe continued to sing Pleasantly in the shower.

***

His breathing was harsh, as he rushed into the bedroom that he shared with his wife. It was almost out of control now. The sweat poured down Jacob's face as he ransacked the room, looking frantically for the bottle.

"Where is it?" He mumbled to himself. "I always keep a spare bottle in here. Where the hell is it?!!" He couldn't control it much longer. He needed to find it.

"That bitch!!" Jacob roared, thinking of his wife as he upturned the dresser chest. "What did that bitch do with it?!! I'll kill her! I'll kill her!!!"

He looked at his hands in shock. The veins were visible and pulsed an ugly black color. His nails had begun to stretch.

"No!!!" Jacob screamed in rage. He ran down the stairs and grabbed his car keys off the table. Running out of the house, he jumped into his car and drove off at breakneck speed.

He had to reach it before it was too late.

***

Phoebe came out of the shower, toweling her hair and thinking of the meat loaf she would make for dinner that night. When she entered her room, nothing could have prepared her for the violence that hit her full force.

Buckling to her knees, she fought for breath as the choking feeling began to recede.

The bedroom was in shambles. The dressers were overturned, the clothes thrown everywhere; the mattress was flung across the room.

Panting, she shakily got to her feet, and slowly walked further into her room. Someone must have entered the house while she was in the shower. Turning in a circle, surveying the area in shock, she put her hands to her head and shook it in confusion.

"How?" She thought out loud to herself. "How could someone have broken in without me knowing?"

Phoebe focused her energy and closed her eyes. She didn't sense anyone in the house. But someone had definitely been there. No matter how hard she tried, she couldn't see who it was. All she could see was darkness. Darkness and indescribable pain. Was she losing her gift? Or was Amanda right? As she walked around the room, she noticed something on the wall.

Her breath caught in her throat, as she stared at it. The coldness and anger in the room could not be mistaken. She could not lie to herself anymore. Not when it affected those she loved.
There, on the wall in bright red, was the bold imprint of a hand smeared in blood. The claws were clearly defined.

It was the unmistakable sign of the devil.

***

Vanessa walked through the front door and immediately felt strangeness.
A funny tingling in her legs and back. She couldn't explain it. It seemed to overtake her. It was like a live ominous presence in her home.

"Mom? Dad?" she walked into the living room cautiously. Everything seemed in order.

"Sweetie, you're home early. I thought you were out with friends."

Vanessa turned at the sound of her mother's voice.

Phoebe stood at the top of the stairs. Her silky hair pulled tightly into its usual bun. She wore loose fitting beige slacks, and a matching blouse. Her mom looked fresh from a shower, however, Vanessa sensed something. Something...dark.

"Mom?" She said nervously, starting up the stairs. "Is everything okay? Where's dad?"

Vanessa swore she thought her mom's face paled. But then Phoebe smiled, and the feeling passed.

"Oh he's not home yet, sweetie. Come on up, I'd like to show you something."

Phoebe turned and went into the room they used as a study. Vanessa followed her mom upstairs, pausing slightly, at her parent's closed bedroom door. A shadow seemed to pass over it. She trembled, sure she was just imaging things.

"Vanessa?" Her mom called to her. Walking into the study, she sat down across from her mother. It was the most comfortable room in the house. Probably because it was her mom's favorite spot. Books lined the walls on top of the shelves. The furniture was spacious, with only a mahogany desk and chair in the middle, and two lounging chairs off to the side. Vanessa's mind wandered. Idly, she wondered where her puppy, 'Spiky', had gone off to. She hadn't seen him since she'd come home. Her mother sat at the desk; her hands folded across it. Focusing her attention back to her, Vanessa frowned. She looked sad, somehow.

"Mom?" She asked softly. "What's wrong?"

Phoebe smiled sadly and stared at her a moment. Lowering her eyes, she opened the desk drawer.

"Honey, there's something I want to give you." She pulled out a long silver box. "I wasn't going to give this to you until your wedding day. Whenever that happy day arrives."

Vanessa blushed profusely, lowering her head in shame. She still had yet to tell her mom about Christopher. She just hadn't seemed to find the right time to do it. Or maybe she was just scared at what she would say.

Phoebe opened the long box and withdrew a beautiful gold locket, shaped in the form of a heart.

Vanessa gasped.

"Oh mom! It's beautiful!" She jumped from her seat and hurried over to her mother, kneeling before her. She touched the glittering necklace. Enraptured, Vanessa opened the locket. Inside was a picture of her mom. She was smiling, and her eyes were laughing and filled with love. There was something written on the inside. She squinted to read it. It said: 'To my Vanessa, From Mommy'. Her eyes watered. She Glanced up at her mom and found that her eyes were filled as well.

"Oh mom!" She threw her arms around Phoebe, and let the tears fall. Her heart expanding in her chest. Phoebe closed her eyes and wrapped her arms around her daughter. Hugging her close. Releasing her, she gently put the necklace around Vanessa's neck.

"I love you. You're my precious little girl."
She stroked her lovely dark hair, closing her eyes against the fear she felt. Against the knowledge of what was to come.

"Always keep it on, baby." Phoebe said to her, looking at the locket gleaming on her daughter's neck. She only prayed that the spell she had cast upon it would withstand the pain.

"Don't ever take it off. It will protect you, always. And so will I."

Vanessa did not question the urgency in her mother's eyes, or even ask why she felt the need for protection.

"I won't mamma." She vowed, smiling and hugging her tightly. Her mother's love washed over her.

"I'll never take it off. I promise."

CHAPTER EIGHT

Jacob raced his car through town. Not caring if he knocked someone over in the street. People ran screaming, trying to rush out of the way of the speeding vehicle. The sweat had now completely soaked his body. He looked as if a bucket of water had been doused over his head. Heading for the woods, he crashed through the trees. Maneuvering the car down the narrow winding path.

Suddenly, it was as if the vehicle had taken on a life of its own, as the wheel began to move by itself. Jacob's eyes widened as he jerked his hands from it, watching the steering wheel twist and turn. The car came to an abrupt halt. Sending him crashing through the windshield. Screaming in pain, he rolled down a hill, breaking his arm and smashing his ribs. A small pond broke his fall. Landing face first into the water, Jacob lay there. Oblivious to anything as darkness took hold of him.

When he came to, he was on his back, lying in the dirt next to the pond. The blood gushed from his head and created a sticky pool beneath him.

Eyes widening, he touched his bloody broken body, and cried out in torment and rage. His voice was that of a thousand screams from hell. Tearing at his body, he stripped off his clothes and raised his hands high into the air and bellowed his rage at the rising moon.

"Why?" He cried out to the darkness.

"Why have you done this to me, master?! I have been faithful to you! I've done everything you've asked me to do! Why do you torment me like this?!!"

The pain came instantly. Jacob fell to his knees, crying and trembling. Small claws began to protrude from his back, lining in rows down his spine. He screeched an inhuman cry, as gashes appeared on his skin.

A long claw mark swiped across his face, as if he'd been scratched viciously, knocking him to the ground. Three long lines of blood appeared on his back, as he writhed and wriggled on his stomach.

"Ask what you will of me!" Jacob spat blood, as his voice screeched and rasped.

"Bring her to me." The voice was silky smooth in his head. Cold, slithering and hypnotic.
"I will wait no longer! Bring her to me now!!"

"Yes." He wept into the ground as he begged for mercy. "Yes, I will bring her to you, master. I will not fail you."

Instantly, the bottle appeared on the ground before him. It was what he'd longed for. His perfection. Jacob grabbed it and ripped the top away. He drank lustfully; it was like a never ending fountain. As he drank, the gashes disappeared from his body, the sweat and blood dried up. The claws retreated; the welts and bruises were gone.

Jacob stood there, naked and feeling powerful, as he watched the windshield on his car renewed.

His hair was once again slicked back and glossy. His elegant dark blue suit materialized onto his body. He felt the smile spread along his face. This was perfection. Without flaw. Without guilt. He, Jacob Dickens, was perfect. It was all he'd ever wanted. All he'd ever craved to be.

He picked up his torn clothes and carried them to the trunk of his car. Placing them in a brown box, he retrieved a shovel that he kept in the trunk and walked with his items to his favorite spot in the woods. He began to shovel the dirt away and soon uncovered the numerous stacks of boxes he'd buried week after week. He couldn't even remember when it had all started. It seemed like it always was. The craving was a part of him now.

And so was the demon.

'Do not fail me.' The voice whispered again. 'If you do, you will die'.

***

Bethany Simpson tucked her children away into bed and kissed them goodnight. Her little girl, Mary, was only five, and her son, Joshua, was seven. They were her world. She didn't know what she would do without them. Switching off the light, she left their room and peeked into her bedroom.

Derek was fast asleep. He'd had a long day at work at the McMann Ranch. She slowly walked into the room and stood next to the bed. Watching him sleep. She loved him so much. He was so strong and stable, when she could be so short sighted at times.

He slept in the nude. His firmly muscled workman's body was exquisite. His loving arms were always so gentle when he held her. Bending over, she gave him a sweet and tender kiss on the lips. She touched his handsome face, loving the way his goatee tickled her. She whispered how much she loved him. He'd been so calm during the storm, when she had discovered her friend was missing.

Leaving the room, she silently closed the door and went downstairs. The town was concerned. She thought bitterly. But as far as she was concerned, they weren't doing enough to find Roselyn.

Entering her husband's office, Bethany sat down at his desk and brooded over things. They'd had a meeting yesterday. The four witches that still followed Phoebe had gathered together for a private meeting. Without Phoebe. It was now a standoff situation. The bi-weekly meetings were canceled, indefinitely. It was down to good versus evil.

Bethany frowned as she thought of Phoebe. Her beloved leader and friend, and the heated discussion that went on in the meeting.

"It has gone too far, Amanda!"

Bethany shouted at the beautiful auburn haired woman. They all saw Amanda as the real second in command. She was a part of Phoebe that none of them quite understood.

"I don't even know why it was allowed to go this far!" Another member of their group called, Crystal, shouted out and flung her hands in the air.

"Amanda, why isn't Phoebe doing anything to stop this?" The fourth member, Barbara, spoke up. "Doesn't she realize what all this could mean?"

"She does realize it." Amanda said, gravely. She stood before them and stared them all in the eye. She faced down their anger in Phoebe's stead.
"She's just not ready to face it yet."

"Well we must make her face it!" Bethany shouted. She jumped up and jabbed a finger into Amanda's chest. "That's my friend out there! And I'm tired of sitting around and waiting for Phoebe to wake up and realize that we have a demon in our midst!!"

Amanda's eyes widened in shock, at her angry words.

"Yes," Bethany said softly, the tears rolling down her cheeks. "We all know, Mandy. We know of the danger that is here. And if we don't do something, right now, someone else is going to die. This time, it might be Phoebe."

Bethany lowered her head onto her husband's desk and wept. Amanda had promised to speak with Phoebe yesterday, and to make her listen to reason.

Although they all knew that it was a lost cause. Phoebe would not listen.

Getting up from the desk, Bethany wiped away her tears, and tore a sheet of paper from her husband's notebook. Quickly, she scribbled a note for him, and left it on the desk.

"I have to do this." She said to herself, as she walked out of the house. If no one else would help her friend, then it was up to her.

She would put an end to this tonight. Getting in her car, Bethany drove to the house in the woods. Everyone knew about the house Carolyn had moved into. And why. It was dark and creepy. Only one light was lit. The trees seemed to dance around the house wickedly. Swallowing down her fear, Bethany got out of her car and walked to the cottage. Just before she knocked on the door, she felt something. Like a pulling.

Bethany suddenly had a strong feeling to leave this place. Like a loud warning screaming in her head. But before she could change her mind, the door opened, and Carolyn Stood there smiling at her.

CHAPTER NINE

"What a pleasant surprise, Bethany."

Carolyn's voice was like silk. Her smile was tempting, and seductive. She was wearing her hair loose, as usual, and was draped in a see-thru long white slip. Everything could be seen.

"Uh, I'm sorry Carolyn if I caught you at a bad time." Said Bethany, her cheeks burned in embarrassment. "I can come back tomorrow during the day."

"Now there's certainly no need for that. Now is as good a time as any." Carolyn pulled her inside and smiled invitingly at her. She walked her down the hall and into the living room. "You're just in time to join the party."

Bethany stopped dead, as she viewed the scene before her. She was a mouse that had innocently walked right into the lion's den.

Kathryn, Sarah, and Amy were all naked. Their limbs twisted around them, as they pleasured each other. Sarah was lavishly devouring Kathryn's breasts. Sucking and biting them. Kathryn's head was on the ground buried between Amy's legs, gripping her buttocks with long red nails. And Amy....Amy was on her knees having oral sex, with Jacob Dickens.

"Oh…my….God…" Bethany's eyes were bulging in shock and dismay, as she stared at Jacob. Phoebe's husband.

"There is no God here, Sweetheart." Carolyn chuckled deviously. "Come, join us." She stepped towards her and lifted a hand to Bethany's shocked face, stroking it gently. But Bethany quickly came out of her paralyzed state and slapped her hand viciously away from her.

"Get the fuck away from me you bitch!!!"
Her outburst brought the attention of everyone in the room. All eyes were suddenly on her, in a room now as silent as death.

"Ahh," Jacob sighed, as he stroked Amy's head like a favored pet. "Fresh meat has arrived."

"What the hell has gotten into you, Jacob?!" Bethany raged at him. "What's going on? How could you do this to Phoebe?" Everyone in the room began to laugh. Everyone except Bethany and Jacob.

"Sweet, sweet foolish Bethany." He spoke the words like a tender caress. "I think you know the answer to that question. Just as I'm sure you know the answer to what happens next."

Bethany realized all too late, that she was trapped. They surrounded her. Carolyn had stripped off her thin slip and was now as naked as the rest of them.

They walked around her in a tight circle. She whirled around, trying to keep them all in sight.

"You know why you came here, sweet Bethany." Carolyn said smoothly, as they circled around her. "You know why Roselyn had to die, and why you must die as well."

"No!!" she tried to run but was shoved back into the circle. Cold laughter rang around her.

"For power," Carolyn continued. "It is all about power. For all I will possess when I kill Phoebe."

"Let me go!!" Bethany tried again to break through the tight circle they had formed.

"You see," Carolyn said softly, "Roselyn knew too much, and she betrayed us. She told you all of our plans. And now, thanks to your friend, you will join her in hell."

"Fuck you!!!" Bethany spat in her face, as the tears rolled down her cheeks. "No matter what you try, you will never succeed!! Roselyn told me everything. Phoebe has something that is above all of us, a gift that none of us can understand. You're nothing compared to her. You will never be Phoebe!"

Carolyn snarled, and yanked Bethany to her, gripping her by the hair painfully. Her red hair was like fire, it made her look as if she was ablaze. Her black eyes were mirrors of rage, as she pulled her face close to hers. Holding her head tight, she kissed her viciously in the mouth, darkly pleased when Bethany struggled to release herself. She could taste her fear and smell the death that was to come. Finally, she broke the kiss and grinned wickedly at her.

"Tonight," She whispered into Bethany's trembling mouth, "You die."

Carolyn slowly traced her tongue over her lips. "But first, we'll have some fun." This time, Bethany was not even allowed to scream.

***

Amanda woke up the next morning with a scream on her lips.

Something was wrong. Something terrible had happened. Jumping out of the bed, she threw on her clothes and didn't waste a moment. She drove all the way to Phoebe's house, a feeling of terror gripping her. Phoebe was just leaving, and looked up, surprised to see her.

"Amanda?" She said, shocked but happy to see her. "What are you doing here?" Without answering, Amanda fired a question of her own.

"Is Jacob home?" Phoebe was taken aback by her friend's attitude.

"Why, no. Of course not. He's already left for the bank."

"Good." Amanda took her arm and dragged her back into the house.

"Amanda what are you doing?! Let go of me!!" Phoebe jerked her arm away in irritation at her friend's behavior. "What's gotten into you?"

"No!!" She spun on her, her auburn hair flying around her shoulders. "What's gotten into you?! Damn it! Your blind, Phoebe!! You walk around totally oblivious to everything!!"

"I'm not—" Phoebe started to deny it, but Amanda cut her off.

"Just shut up!!" She was through being patient. "There are lives at stake here, Phoebe. Your promise is broken. You let in those who were unworthy. Ignoring the consequences." She continued on as she backed her into a chair.

"You took an oath to protect. But all you've protected is yourself! Hiding away in fear. Refusing to show your family who you really are. You lie to them, and you lie to the town, but you cannot lie to yourself! You cannot lie to me!!"

Amanda was trembling in rage and fury. Fear and pain, lies and mistrust were all pent up within her. She could not take it anymore. She couldn't take Phoebe not accepting who she truly was. One who could fly to the moon, or dance with the stars. One who held so much power tapped deep within her. But she denied it. Pretending to be like everyone else. It was going to be her downfall.

And that was what Amanda feared most.

"Have you even told Vanessa the truth?" She asked her. Phoebe's eyes widened at the mention of her daughter's name.

"Leave her out of this!" She shouted, starting to get up.

"She is part of it!!" Amanda shouted back at her, pushing her back down into the chair. "Do you even know that your daughter is in love, and has been since the start of summer?"

Phoebe's eyes watered in confusion. The hurt and pain was evident in them.

"But...but that can't be..." She stammered, "I would have known...."

"No. You wouldn't Phoebe." Amanda said softly. She never could take seeing her hurt. "What is plain to everyone else does not exist to you. You can see it in her eyes. And in the way she walks. She's in love with someone, and you should be talking to her about it. But you've shut down."

Amanda sighed and sank onto the couch.

"All the things that have happened, Roselyn, your husband, and now Bethany."

Before Phoebe could ask what she'd meant about her husband, her whole body went still.

"What's happened to Bethany?" She flung the words at her. Her blood had suddenly turned to ice. Before she could answer, Phoebe jumped up. Her face was white as a ghost.

"No…no!" She shouted. Before she could stop her, Phoebe ran out of the house.

Amanda ran after her.

"Phoebe wait!!" But she'd already jumped in her vehicle.

"I'm sorry, Mandy." She whispered to herself, as she reversed the car, the tears shining in her eyes. "But I have to do this alone. I have to help Bethany."

She drove off with a screech of tires. Amanda looked after her, the tears falling from her face. No way was she going to let her do this alone. Just then, as she turned to head for her own car, she stopped cold, as she spotted Vanessa standing in the doorway. Her face was just as pale as Phoebe's had been. It was like looking into a mirror.

"Is it true?" Vanessa whispered, staring at the woman whom she considered as an aunt.

Amanda's heart sank, as she stared at the girl she loved like a daughter.

Her suspicions had been correct. Phoebe had never told her the truth.

And Vanessa had overheard everything.

CHAPTER TEN

Phoebe drove as fast as she could to the Simpson house.

"Please, let her be alright." She prayed silently. But she knew nothing would ever be right again. If only she had listened. She berated herself, slamming her hand on the dashboard in frustration, blinking away the tears that blurred her vision.

Pulling up in front of the house she saw that half the town was already gathered there, swarming on the front lawn. Some walking in and out of the house.

Jumping out of her car Phoebe ran up the porch steps, ignoring the people who called out to her. Entering, she saw that there was chaos. The children were nowhere to be seen, and at least ten men and women were standing around Derek, who was sitting on the sofa.

Everyone was talking at once, arguing and gesturing at him. But as soon as they saw her, all conversation stopped. Their eyes held regret as they stared. Slowly they made a path, allowing her to go to him.

Derek sat on the couch with his head in his hands, weeping like a lost child; a crumpled piece of paper was clutched in his left hand. Phoebe's heart ripped in two. She was too late.

Going over to him, she knelt before him and gently placed her hand on his arm.

Derek glanced up. His face was Ravaged and worn from tears. His eyes were blood shot and empty. A look of hopelessness swam in them. As his gaze focused on her, his eyes seemed to change. They became darker, his pupils becoming smaller as they registered her.

Phoebe knew it was inevitable. She wasn't even sure that she didn't deserve it.

His fist shot out like a lightning bolt and slammed against her face with such force, that she was knocked across the room.

Shouting ensued as Phoebe was helped to her feet by the women, the room spinning as she fought not to black out. The men held down Derek as he thrashed around violently, looking at her with a crazed expression on his face.

"You killed her!! You killed my wife!! If it wasn't for you, she'd still be alive!! You're the one that deserves to die! You are!!!" The men carried him away, as he fought and screamed.

Phoebe stood in the room. A trickle of blood trailed down her lip.

Derek's words echoing straight through to her soul. The truth of it, was that more damning.

She had betrayed her coven. She had betrayed the vows she'd sworn to uphold. She did not deserve to live. Without another word, Phoebe turned and dashed out of the room.

She was oblivious to the people who shouted after her, tried to stop her. She could no longer hear anyone. She knew what she had to do. Not bothering to take the car, she ran.

All her life, she had known who she was. And that her duty was to protect. To watch over what was in her care, and to guard her secrets. But she had wanted so much to be like everyone else. To just be normal.

She had deluded herself to the point where she'd even lied to her own daughter.

Her hair fell out of its pins as she ran. The wind whipping through her long purple dress.
Somehow, she would make things right. Panting, she entered the woods.

All sound and motion stopped. The trees seemed to close in around her, as if they'd been waiting for her.

"At last, she has arrived."

The sultry voice wrapped around her like a seductive evil blanket.

"Carolyn." Phoebe uttered the name like a curse.

"I've waited a long time for this." Carolyn replied in satisfaction.

She came out of the shadows and smiled wickedly at Phoebe. She was wearing an all black tight leather body suit, and her lips were a fiery red that matched her hair.

"So long to have a taste of what you have, beautiful Phoebe."

She tensed, as Carolyn came closer. She was like a cat, playing with the mouse. Her eyes narrowed.

"What have you done with my friends?" She flung the words at her.

"Oh, you mean Rosie, and Bethie?" Carolyn chuckled. "Oh, I killed them. They were such enjoyable amusements. Especially Bethany."

She was now face to face with Phoebe.

"I just loved the way she tried to scream for her life."

The hot flash of pain came so suddenly, that Carolyn barely had time to cry out. Trembling violently, she fell to her knees. Her eyes rolled to the back of her head, as the painful spasms wracked her body.

"And now, you will scream for yours." Phoebe said with deadly calm.

She raised her arms high above her head. Suddenly the sky grew dark, and lightening shot across it.

"It's over, Carolyn." She prepared the death blow.

"I don't think so, darling."
That voice, so smooth, so charming, was her one fatal mistake.

"J...Jacob?" Phoebe lowered her arms and turned to face him. He stood a few feet away from her. As handsome and dashing as always. Her heart melted at the sight of him. She took a tentative step towards him.

"Honey, please...let me help you."

When Jacob said nothing, she frowned and took another step towards him, and realized too late, that it was a trap. Phoebe fell screaming into a large hole that had been covered with grass. It was the size of a grave, and just as deep. A hole she would've known was there, had her emotions not been clouded. It had blinded her. Just as Amanda had said it did.
She landed hard on the ground, bruising her arm and legs.

Crying out in pain, she struggled to get up.

"Jacob!" She screamed up at him, tears of frustration stinging her eyes.

"Jacob don't do this!"

He stared down at her, his eyes glazed and shining. A demonic glow swam within their depths. Phoebe gasped in fear and dismay. How could she not have seen it? Her body trembled.

"My sweet wife," Jacob lowered himself onto his stomach, and leaned over the edge of the hole. "You never even knew me."

He said it with revulsion, a cruel smile spreading across his face.

"I have planned for so long and waited so patiently for this day to come. You and your secrets that you have never been able to hide from me. I have always known!!"

Jacob shouted into the grave. His hands fisting in fury.

"I wanted to destroy the very thing that made you what you are. And now, I've been given the perfect opportunity. The perfect reward, to dispose of something I never wanted."

Phoebe shook her head in denial, her eyes wide with terror, still not wanting to believe that all this time she'd been loving and living with a demon.

"He came to me, my love." Jacob whispered reverently. "He came to me and offered me new life.

He offered me perfection. All I had to do was destroy you. Release within you, that which my master craves."

His eyes widened with Dementia.

"He told me you have the key, and today, with the help of Carolyn, is the day I will claim it."

"No!!" Phoebe cried. She backed up into the wall of the grave, fighting the panic and fear.
She knew exactly what he meant. She knew what he was after.

"And when I'm through with you," Jacob left the best for last, "I'm going to take much pleasure in comforting our beautiful sweet daughter." He smiled deviously.

"And making her mine."

Phoebe almost lost control then. She screamed in fury clawing at the dirt, trying to free herself. But she couldn't channel her powers if she couldn't Focus. Her emotions were blocking her way. And that was exactly as Jacob wanted it.

"Ah, women." Carolyn's seductive laugh reached her ears as she looked down at her.

"You know Phoebe, for someone so powerful, you sure are pathetically weak." She snickered as she shared an open mouthed kiss with Jacob.

As phoebe watched them, she felt the last of her hope die away.

"Shall we begin my love?" said Carolyn.

"Oh yes." Jacob smiled at her. He withdrew a bottle from his suit jacket and shook the contents into the hole with Phoebe. As she screamed in agony, he smiled pleasantly.

"Let us begin."

***

Jacob, Carolyn, Kathryn, and Sarah all climbed into the hole with the unconscious Phoebe. Jacob had tied a rope to a tree, and Amy remained above to keep watch.

"Do you think it will work?" Carolyn asked him, as she knelt down next to Phoebe.

"It will. When she awakens, she will be too disoriented to use her power. She needs to focus in order for them to work.

"Yes." She reached out and stroked a hand down Phoebe's beautiful body. "I have always wanted a taste of what she has."

"Let's get on with it." Kathryn mumbled jealously. Sarah grinned at her knowingly.

Slowly, Carolyn stripped Phoebe of all her clothes. Relishing at the sight of her nudity, bared for her view at last. Sarah held her left arm down, and Kathryn held the right. Jacob remained at the foot of her, holding down her legs. He began to chant, as they started the ritual. Carolyn stripped out of her own outfit and climbed on top of her. She began to stroke her, kiss her, massaging her body as she danced and moved.

Phoebe began to awaken. She didn't know what was going on. Her body felt weighted down.
It was burning all over. Slowly opening her eyes, she saw all of them above her. Their faces blurring out of focus. Someone was on top of her, doing things to her body. But it wasn't Jacob.... Jacob.

"Wait....stop!" She tried to get a hold of her thoughts, tried to focus, but she couldn't. Her body was pinned. There was evil laughter all around her, and a deep monotone chanting. Someone was touching her, licking her body.

"No! please!" She felt herself slipping into a strange hypnotic state, as the chanting grew louder.

"Give me what I want, Phoebe." The sultry voice was above her.

"Give me what you possess!"

"Never!!" Phoebe screamed, fighting the haze, drowning in a sea of confusion and delirium. She had to keep hold of the one thing she knew would help her focus.

Amanda.

"Give it to me!!"

Carolyn raged. She slapped her viciously, once, twice, again and again. Phoebe's head jerked from side to side, blood spilled from her mouth.

"Give it to me, you bitch!!" She took a whip she'd brought with her and began to beat her with it. Slashing Phoebe's body again and again until blood gushed everywhere.

Still, Carolyn continued to mutilate her, even as her screams wrenched through the woods, she did not stop.

Jacob sighed impatiently.

"It won't do us any good if someone hears her."

"Well we don't have anything to shut her mouth with." Said Sarah, her eyes were gleaming in excitement, and her body was aroused from watching Phoebe writhe in pain.

As Carolyn stared at her, she realized with building fury, that Phoebe was never going to willingly give up the key. Bleeding, and half conscious, Phoebe looked up at her.

92

Though she was nearly dead, she thought of her daughter, and of Amanda. And all that she had lost. Her rage sparked one last time, and she closed it off. Shutting down what was inside of her, protecting those she loved one final time. For if it was ever released, or used the wrong way, the thought was inconceivable.

She stared up into Carolyn's evil face and smiled weakly. Accepting her fate.

"You will never have what I control."

She whispered weakly.

"Go to hell."

Carolyn shrieked in rage as she joined her mouth to Phoebe's and viciously, with claw like teeth, ripped out her tongue.

As she felt herself giving way to the pain, her eyes watched as each of them climbed out of the grave. Carolyn threw something on her. It felt like water. It was cold as it splashed on her skin.

As Carolyn's arm flung into the air for a second time, Phoebe watched as a small object fell into the hole with her. Erupting her, and the entire grave into a raging inferno.

Thankfully, she could not feel her body burn as the onlookers stood above her and watched her die.

Her only thought, as the bed of flames surrounded her, was of Amanda.

CHAPTER ELEVEN

Vanessa stared at Amanda as she tried to take in everything she'd just told her.

She sat on the sofa in the living room of her house and looked around. Her eyes were dazed. Why didn't her mother ever tell her the truth?

"Why did she lie to me?" Vanessa flung the question at Amanda. Tears brimming in her eyes.

"Why did she just let me go through all of these changes, and become ridiculed at school, and not tell me why?!"

Amanda's heart ached for her. She wished that she could wipe away the pain and hurt that she saw in her eyes.

"She wanted to sweetie, but your mom has not been herself lately. She lost sight of who she was. And who you are." She went to her, sat down on the sofa and took hold of her hands.

"You have a gift, Vanessa. It is not a curse. No matter what anyone may try to make you feel."

Amanda felt the regret rise up to choke her. Vanessa should've been taught from birth about who and what she was. Just as she'd learned how to walk, she should've been taught how to channel her power, to use it only for good. And most of all, how to focus and dilute her anger. She was already sixteen. Nearly a full grown woman set in her ways. It would be hard to teach her now, but she would leave that up to Phoebe.

"Do you have it?"

Amanda was startled out of her thoughts, at the abrupt question.

"Do I have what sweetie?"

Vanessa Sighed impatiently.

"You know. The gift. Like me and mom."

Amanda's smile froze in place at the direct question. Gingerly, she shied away from it.

"Honey, these are really questions that you need to ask your mom." She started to turn away, but Vanessa grabbed her arm in frustration.

"Don't treat me this way, Aunt Mandy!" She cried. "Don't treat me like I don't have a right to know!"

Amanda sighed in resignation, as she read the pleading look in her eyes.

"Alright. You'll probably need something to drink." She leaned back into the couch, and Amanda went to go pour them some juice.

Coming back with their glasses, she handed one to
Vanessa sitting down across from her. She took her
time getting settled, sipping her drink and giving
herself a chance to relax a bit.

Amanda prayed Phoebe didn't kill her for what she
was about to say.

"Me and your mother share a very deep secret."
She began, taking a deep breath.

"No one knows about this. And even if they did,
they would not believe you." She paused.
Vanessa's body began to tense. She had a feeling that
what she was about to hear, was monumental.
Amanda continued.

"A long time ago, your mom was just like you.
Confused. Not really wanting to accept who she was.
She just wanted to be a normal girl. She'd lived in
Melrose since she was seven years old, and since she
was the new girl and nobody knew her or her mom,
the kids were very cruel. She was an only child, and
her dad had died when she was very young. So it was
just her and her mom."

"I never knew my grandmother."
Vanessa said softly.

"She was a beautiful woman, with a heart of gold."
Said Amanda, her eyes watering.
"She died in a car accident one night, many years
ago. Your mom was only ten years old."

She paused as the familiar pain took root in her heart.

"Your mother was completely alone. All she had was her gift. She was taken to an orphanage miles away from Melrose. Again, she was treated cruelly. But her mother had taught her well, how to control her rage." She sighed. "But she wanted more. Needed more. And so…" She looked her straight in the eyes.

"She cast a spell on herself."

Vanessa's eyes widened in shock.

"On herself? What did she do?"

Amanda looked across the spacious living room and stared out the window.

"The spell of splitting the spirit." She got up and walked around the room, needing movement. "It was complicated, and it could have killed her. But she was willing to take the risk."

She turned around and watched Vanessa, needing to see her face.

"She split herself in two. Not physically. She created a spell that would take the deeper part of her soul and form it into a living breathing entity. If one was to die, technically, she was still alive because the other part of her lived. Not just in the mind, but in the body as well."

Amanda stuffed her hands into the pockets of her jeans.

"I was given life at ten years old. Not that I hadn't been alive before, I was always there. Living and breathing as Phoebe. As part of her subconscious, so to speak. But it was like I was suddenly given independence. To be able to go where I want, do what I want, and just be a separate being."

The tension in Amanda's body was evident.

"But I always was, and always will be, Phoebe. It's like two of us walking around."

Her jaw clenched in frustration, as she thought of the very important details she was leaving out. Phoebe had done more than deny who she was. She had created a false image, pretending to be a witch, when she knew she was so much more.

Vanessa stared at Amanda as if she'd grown two heads.

"Are you serious?" She asked, incredulously. "How could that be? Wouldn't you guys feel the same things? Know the same things?"

She jumped up and threw her hands in the air.
"What if one of you got hurt? Wouldn't the other feel it as well?"

Before Amanda could respond, a burning so hot, made her fall to her knees. She began to shake violently, her skin beading with sweat. She looked at her hands as her veins seemed to writhe to the point of bursting. Her arms looked as though they were melting before her very eyes.

"Mandy!! Aunt Mandy what's wrong? What's happening to you?!!"

Vanessa rushed over to her.

Amanda couldn't hear her.

The burning. It was so hot. So terrible. She knew what was happening. And she couldn't stop it. She felt the tears scorch her face, as she threw back her head and lifted her arms in impotent rage.

"Phoebe!!!" She screamed as the burning seared her.

"Phoebe, nooo!!!!!!"

CHAPTER TWELVE

The funerals were held in the community center at the end of town. Everyone in Melrose, and a few from surrounding farms, was in attendance. The three Brown coffins stood in rows placed at the front of the congregation. The caskets lay open to display the still bodies lying prone and cold within them.

Vanessa watched as the women who called themselves witches, were the first to approach the coffins, and pay their respects. She watched as Crystal and Barbara joined hands with Amanda, as they stared down at their closest friends. The tears slowly streaked down Amanda's cheeks.

Vanessa looked away, unable to bear it. She remained at the back of the center, apart from everyone. Unwilling to join in the mourning of the onlookers gathered before her. She felt the familiar rage try to build up within her. With an effort, she willed the pain away. It was better to not feel at all, than to feel everything.

A low murmur went through the crowd, and Vanessa's attention was again drawn to the front, where four other women had joined the small group of mourners lined by the caskets.

This time, she was unable to control her fury.

Carolyn walked into the center, boldly. Her tall shapely body was draped in a tight black dress that hugged her every curve and dip. Her black high heels clicked on the hardwood floor, as she walked over to Phoebe's coffin. Her flaming hair was left to flow like silk, down her back. Her breasts were accentuated with every move she made. A dark veil covered the evil pleasure that shone on her face. Her smile was wicked, and cold. All talking stopped as she, Kathryn, Amy, and Sarah reached the caskets.

Taking a slow glance at Amanda's stricken face, Carolyn looked down at Phoebe's lifeless form. Grinning, she bent over the coffin and kissed the cold lips.

"So how is it in hell?"

She whispered into Phoebe's frozen mouth. No one but Amanda heard the softly spoken words. Straightening, Carolyn turned and watched in amusement, as Amanda's eyes began to glaze with outrage.

"How dare you!!" She shouted. The dull crack of her jaw could be heard across the large room, as Amanda punched her solidly in the face. Carolyn's body was thrown across the center by force of the impact, crashing into a row of chairs.

The people scrambled out of the way. Total chaos erupted. The witches of Melrose began an all out battle. Punching and slapping.

Using chairs on each other to inflict mortal pain, and worse. It was obvious that the outcome would be death.

The sound of a gunshot blasted through the ceiling of the community center. Someone screamed, everyone was startled into stillness.

Mr. Gerard Lawson, the owner of the liquor store on Main Street, stood in the doorway. A large rifle braced in his hands.

"That's what happens when you let in a bunch of women who think they're witches, in a town with no damn law!"

His gravelly voice boomed into the silence. Mr. Lawson was a large man. His huge stomach protruded past his waist, and his arms were masses of fat rolled together. His thick head sat on a neck that remained to be seen, and his cheeks hung on his face like long floppy pieces of skin, earning him the nickname Bulldog.

Lowering the gun, he stomped into the center and shoved past the people. Reaching the coffins, he looked at the bodies, and then shot a quick look of animosity towards the seven women who had scrambled to their feet.

"This here town aint' been nothin' but trouble since you women started your damn occult group!"

Carolyn swiped the blood from the side of her mouth and slyly assessed Bulldog. The townspeople had begun to gather behind him, staring at them. She knew his voice held a lot of weight. The people respected him and saw him as the town's hired gun. As he was the biggest, and the toughest, he was always given a wide berth.

She watched him with cold calculating eyes. Now was not the time to make an enemy of this one.

"We are not at fault here." Carolyn's voice held just the right amount of tremor, to catch her audience. Her southern accent was overly emphasized, as her eyes widened in feigned pain and hurt. Her veil had been ripped off in her tussle with Amanda. There was a long red scratch on her cheek and a dark purple bruise, where she'd been punched. Her hair was in disarray about her face.

The slow tear that trickled down her cheek, all added to the effect of the perfectly injured lady. Slowly, knowing all eyes were on her, Carolyn withdrew a silky black handkerchief from between her firm, voluptuous creamy bosom. Her breasts were sitting on display for her viewers, straining against the material of her dress. Her nipples were barely covered.

The men began to drool hungrily, as she used the handkerchief to slowly wipe away the tear, and then very seductively, began to gently mop the gleaming sheen of sweat that covered each bulging breast.

104

Carolyn watched Bulldog as his eyes lustfully followed her every move.

No. She thought pleasantly to herself. He wouldn't be too hard to handle at all.

"It seems to me that the ones at fault here, are the ones responsible for the death of these three women."

A stern voice cut into the web of seduction. Carolyn turned towards Mrs. Basely, the grocery store owner, her eyes flashed her a deadly warning. Mrs. Basely met her glare head on and continued.

"It seems we've all forgotten just where we are." Her voice took on that of a teacher scolding a child. "This may be a community center, but it's still a house of God and a funeral is in process. Now you all better show some respect to the lord and let the dead rest in peace!"

Shoving past everyone, old Mrs. Basely approached the caskets. A frown formed on her wrinkled face, and the fear she fought not to reveal crept through her body.

She looked down at Phoebe's beautiful still face. Thinking of the lovely eyes that would never open again. The voice that would never ring with laughter into her store. She'd known her since she was a little girl. And though she'd always given her a hard time, was always barking at her young daughter Vanessa, she'd loved them both. Like family.

You made this town. Mrs. Basely thought to herself, as she stroked Phoebe's cold cheek. But you were always too kind. Too trusting. Wanted everyone in the world to be just as loving as you were. It now has cost you your own life.

The terror returned full force, as Mrs. Basely glanced at the two other still forms. There was a killer in their little non-descript, simple town. A town too small to even warrant a sheriff. If they were to ever need assistance, the state troopers would have to be called in. And it was very unlikely they would be taken seriously. Since the town was built over thirty years ago, there had never been more than a hundred people in population. Some had even moved away. But the number never grew. There wasn't any real attraction to Melrose.

The people who stayed became a part of her. Often believing Melrose was a town apart from anything, or place on earth. And that is how it was treated. Often ignored by outsiders and overlooked and forgotten by Government officials.

Mrs. Basely had lived a majority of her life in Melrose. Through all of the years, there had never been so much as a crime there.

Phoebe had left the orphanage in Raleigh, North Carolina, and had returned to Melrose at the young age of eighteen. She'd brought several young women with her, and they'd later all started their coven. Mrs. Basely had been against it from the start. She knew that Phoebe had a gift; however, she'd always suspected that she and her mother were so much more than witches. It was as if they were hiding something. But she'd strongly believed it was more denied, than hidden.

She felt that starting a witch's coven would only bring trouble. But Phoebe had insisted that witches were only the names they called themselves for their organization. She formed a group of ladies who had caring spirits, and for a time, it was like having personal doctors in Melrose.

It was a far cry better than having to travel miles to the nearest hospital, whenever someone was sick. Mrs. Basely had grudgingly begun to accept that the women Phoebe had taught to heal, and nurture were good at what they did. But she knew she kept her true gifts hidden from them. None of the women had known about Phoebe's true talent, and Mrs. Basely knew that was the way she had wanted it.

Her eyes watered, as she remembered the night she had fallen down the stairs, while she'd been getting ready to retire to bed. It had been past midnight, and she knew no one would hear her, even if she'd been able to scream. Mrs. Basely had accepted her fate, as the pain wracked her frail body. That was when the door had burst open. And though it was a cold stormy night in the middle of winter, Phoebe had rushed into her home, soaking wet. Mrs. Basely didn't have to call out to her, she'd come right into the hallway and rushed to her aide.

"It's alright, Mrs. Basely." Phoebe had said softly, kneeling down beside her. Gentle hands lifted her effortlessly into her arms. She didn't know how she'd done it and had never spoken of it or told anyone of that night. But as soon as Phoebe touched her, Mrs. Basely had felt a warm glow spread throughout her body. All of her pain had vanished instantly. She'd known then that she was not like the rest of them. She wasn't a witch as she would have everyone believe.

She was something else.

Mrs. Basely quietly held her emotions inside, as the townspeople watched her say a silent prayer for the women who had lost their lives. Bowing their heads and falling into a respectful silence. As she spoke the words and looked upon the face of the beautiful woman she had loved like a daughter, she felt the presence of the evil that stood only a few feet away from her.

Watching. And waiting.

CHAPTER THIRTEEN

Christopher McMann stared solemnly at his father from across the table. They sat in silence as usual, as they ate dinner late that evening.

Robert McMann shoveled his food into his mouth, oblivious to anything or anyone else.

He was a hard man, tall, with tightly toned muscles. He wore a beard neatly trimmed, and straight, short cropped dark brown hair. His nose was slightly crooked from one too many fights, and his eyes were the color of chestnuts.

Christopher knew he'd gotten his characteristics and handsome looks mostly from his mother. His mother had been a beautiful tall brunette. Funny, loud, and with a heart as big as the sky.

She died only last year from a strange disease that could not be cured. His jaw clenched as he removed thoughts of his mother from his mind. Since her death, his father had turned into a ruthless hard driving man. Forgetting his son's existence. All traces of love and laughter were brutally removed from the McMann ranch.

Christopher had found himself seeking comfort elsewhere. Going through women like water. Careless of their feelings, until Vanessa Dickens.

A beautiful girl in a town, that almost all his friends had jokingly named, 'The town to nowhere.' Never in his wildest dreams, did he believe he would find such a rose buried within that place. And now that he'd found her, he was determined to keep her.

His blood ran cold as he remembered what he'd overheard that morning from one of the ranch hands. About the mysterious murders going on in Melrose.

He didn't know what was going on over there, or why Vanessa hadn't said anything to him about it. But he was determined at whatever the cost, to get her out of there.

He cleared his throat loudly to gain his father's attention. In the huge dining room, with only two occupants, the sound echoed off the walls.

"What the hell wrong with your throat, boy?!"
His father barked without glancing up.
He continued to shovel food into his mouth.

"I'm getting married."

The simple statement was like a bullet. It pierced through Robert's tough wall of cold disinterest. Choking violently on his food, he slammed his hands on the table. Shaking the dishes and silverware.

"What the hell you done did now, boy!!!" His voice bellowed across the room. Spittle spewing from his mouth.

"You gone and got some tramp knocked up?!!"

Christopher stared at his father's face. His body still, while the fury built within him.

"I'm merely informing you of the decision I've already made."

His voice was hard as granite.

"I don't need your permission or your approval to do so." He scraped his chair back and stood up to leave the room.

"It's that girl, isn't it?"

His father's words stopped him cold.

"That little witch over there in the town of death!!"

Robert McMann didn't know his son could move that fast. Before he realized it, he was on his back flat on the ground. His son's hand was gripped around his neck, squeezing painfully. Christopher's eyes were filled with rage and hate, as he stared at the man he once called father.

"If you ever speak of my wife to be in that tone again, I'll kill you." His words, said with deadly calm, melted the anger that simmered in his father. As Robert looked in his son's eyes, true fear began to take place of the anger. Not for himself, but for his son.

He knew that look. It was all too familiar to him. Like a long ago dream or nightmare.
He had gotten rid of it. It was gone. Or he had thought it was. But as he looked at his son, he knew he hadn't forgotten a thing. It was like a deep seeded wound that would never quite heal. No matter what he had done to destroy it.

The ache intensified, as he remembered. If only things had been different. But they weren't. And his son had to know the truth. Even if he couldn't tell him all of it.

Unfortunately, his son had to discover the rest on his own. That was how he had found out.
He could only hope that when that day came, Christopher would be prepared for the horrifying truth of their destiny.

"Stay away from her, Chris." His father said quietly. His eyes were wide with real terror. "You have no idea what you're getting into."

Christopher hesitated. The look in his father's eyes unnerved him. He'd never seen him so frightened. He released him and stalked away in disgust.

"I know exactly what I'm getting into. It's something called love. Something you've lost sight of ever since mom died!!"

Ice swept through Robert's body. His face darkened with a coldness born of pain and despair. He rose to stand and face his son.

112

"You've got no right to speak to me of love." His voice changed. Christopher could hear the hurt mixed with pain. Robert's heart hardened. Chasing away the memories of torment.

"There aint' no such thing as love when it comes to those Melrose witches!!" His father growled.

"Take heed to my words, boy! That girl is using you as a meal ticket. A pawn for whatever scheme she's cooked up. And if you're lucky," Robert's eyes shone with fear and pain, "You'll escape with your life."

Christopher slammed the doors to the dining room and strode angrily out of the house. His thoughts were dark, as he jumped into his car and headed for Melrose. All he wanted right now was Vanessa. He had no idea what she was going through trapped in such a place, but he knew she needed him.

***

Vanessa stood on the grass, watching from afar as the last coffin was placed into the ground. Her mother's. The caskets were buried in the small town cemetery, situated directly behind the community center. A large fenced in area was sectioned off for this purpose only.

An emptiness seemed to take hold of her, as she stared at the people gathered around the graves. Amanda had told her many things that she still could not comprehend or believe.

Her mother had a special gift, and so did she.

Turning away as the last words were said, the dirt thrown into the ground, Vanessa began to walk silently down the road. Her low heels echoed on the concrete of the empty streets. Mostly everyone had attended the funeral. The town was in shock. They were in fear of the recent events that had taken place. The deaths could no longer be construed as accidents.

It was murder.

She frowned as she walked slowly, looking down at her feet, not caring where she ended up. Her long black dress reached almost down to her ankles and blew in the gentle breeze. Her heartbeat began to race as she remembered only three days ago, Amanda's face burning with redness.
Her screams ripping through the house.

She had passed out. Vanessa had tried to revive her, but her skin had been scalding hot. She had run to the next door neighbors for help. When Amanda had come to, she had wept and thrashed like a madman, screaming Phoebe's name.

Vanessa trembled, remembering how she'd looked, and balled her hands into fists.
She did not notice the wind picking up, or how the trees swung violently as she passed.

It was later discovered that Amanda had known Phoebe was dead. Somewhere in the woods.

114

The men had formed a small search party. What they found had left no doubt in anyone's mind as to what they were facing.

Her body Began to heat up. She didn't know that her eyes had become dark holes of flames. Or that her fists sparked and sizzled.

Two men had found her mother's body, a charred burnt skeleton that was only identified by the wedding ring that remained on her finger. Bethany Simpson and Roselyn Jackson's butchered and head less forms had lain next to it. On either side of her. The two men who'd found the corpses had claimed this was how they'd seen them. However, after they had run off to gather everyone else and help retrieve the bodies, when they returned, the three women were found in the grave. Dead, but whole. Their skin, body and limbs, were all intact.

As the bodies were retrieved, naked and motionless, they had looked as if they were sleeping. The other men in the search party had reported. No traces of injury or cause of death could be seen. The two men that swore to what they had seen earlier had taken their families the next day and left town. They had shouted that anyone who stayed was calling their own death.

Vanessa was unaware that her face was soaked with tears. Or that her feet burned holes into the ground as she walked.

Only she knew the truth. She knew what Amanda had done. She'd watched the burns appear on Amanda's body, as she'd taken them from Phoebe's. She'd stared in silent horror, watching her press her lips together to keep from screaming in morbid pain, as she'd pieced together Bethany and Roselyn's limbs. And she'd done it all, while lying in Vanessa's bed, as the searchers had left to go find Phoebe. And to her utter amazement, she had seen.

Vanessa had seen through Amanda's eye's what she was doing. Fixing and repairing the bodies, so that their souls would not wander. Amanda's eyes had blazed, and fire had burst from her mouth. Flying into the ceiling and disappearing. She had looked at her, and Vanessa had known she was staring at her mother.

The earth trembled as Vanessa entered the woods. She stopped and looked up, immediately feeling the difference here. The terror. The fear. Turning in circles, she heard the laughter.

The echo of the fire and flames.

"Stop it!" She screamed, running deeper into the woods. The voices followed her.
"Leave me alone!!" She shouted into the air, flinging her fists at things she couldn't see.

"Vanessa." She heard her mother's voice calling for her.

"Vanessa." She heard her father's soothing whisper.

"No!" She ran. The dark shapes twisting and turning around her. She could hear the death cries of the three women who'd been murdered, whose blood had been spilled. She felt hands grab her.

"Let go of me!!" Vanessa fought viciously.

"Vanessa! Vanessa!"

Christopher tried to calm her, as he held her tightly in his arms. Finally recognizing his voice, she looked into his familiar loving eyes, and sank pitifully against him. The sobs wracking her body.

He held her, as the voices of death receded.

CHAPTER FOURTEEN

Jacob sat in his office in the small bank he owned, and slowly leaned back in his chair. He couldn't have been in a better mood. Everything was going as planned. It was late into the evening, and the people of Melrose were almost certainly well shut away in their little non-existent holes that they called home. His eyes glinted with amusement.

Did they really think he'd been successful all these years on just their money alone? Fools! He had big plans for this pathetic town. He was secretly working with Investors from all over the world. Plans of making Melrose into the most prosperous city in North Carolina.

In which he would be mayor. Yes. Jacob smiled at the idea. Now, with Phoebe out of the way, it was only a matter of time. And he could finally concentrate on his lovely daughter.

"We've got a problem, Jacob."

His thoughts were interrupted as he turned his focus on Carolyn, sitting across from him. She crossed her smooth long legs, and her tight red skirt hiked up even farther, showing a tantalizing view of her thighs. She tossed her hair over her shoulder and eyed him knowingly.

Watching as his eyes glanced over her body with disinterest. She knew he didn't mind a little play, but he only wanted one person. She frowned as she thought of Phoebe's beautiful daughter.

"We do not have a problem, my dear." He drawled lazily. "Everything is going as planned."

"Don't be a fool!" Carolyn spat the words at him viciously. She got up and paced the office. "You're overlooking the obvious, Jacob, dear." She turned to him and leaned over his desk. Her breasts nearly spilling out of her tight shirt.

"We didn't leave those bodies like that." She said softly, her voice held a note of warning. A dangerous glint sparked in her eyes.

Jacob's smile slowly disappeared. His body growing still, as Carolyn easily reminded him of the one detail he'd blocked from his mind.

He'd seen the bodies when he attended the funeral earlier that day. They were perfect. He hadn't wanted to face the blatant evidence before his eyes. His blood ran cold and his heartbeat began to race.

"My wife was a witch." He said smoothly. "She probably was able to contrive some last spell to heal their bodies."

Carolyn sat on the edge of his desk and looked down at him. The look on her face spoke volumes.

119

"If she still had the power to heal their flesh, she would've used that to save them all, when we threw Roselyn and Bethany's bodies into the fire with her, don't you think?"

Jacob's silence said it all.

Carolyn tapped her fingers slowly on the desk.

"Phoebe succeeded in several things. One, she was more powerful than any of us could have imagined. Even with her death, we were unable to gain access to the key she held within her."

She slammed her fist onto the desk in rage.

"Hey!" Jacob shouted. Carolyn ignored him.
"You said she needed to focus! You swore that all we needed to do was break her, and the power would be released to us!!"

Suddenly, Jacob remembered his master's warning. He could not fail.

"No." He stood up and went to the window. Trying to hide his fear. He swung on Carolyn, needing to place the blame on anyone but himself.

"You told me you knew what you were doing! It was up to you to retrieve the key!!"

"You son of a bitch!! " She whirled on him in fury. "Don't you dare blame me for your fuck up!! This is your fault!"

Just as they were about to leap and tear each other to shreds, the door opened and Sarah walked into the office. She leaned against the wall and lit up a cigarette.

Her tight jeans hugged every part of her, and her shirt buttons were left halfway open to display her ample breasts. Slowly, very nonchalantly, she looked up at them as she puffed out smoke and smiled seductively. She knew she had their attention.

"It wasn't her." She said the words so calmly, that it took Carolyn a moment to understand their meaning.

"What are you talking about, Sarah?" She said, walking over and putting her hands on her hips. "If you've got something to say, you better damn well say it."

Sarah took her time.

She loved to watch Carolyn when she was mad. Softly, she blew smoke into her face.

"Phoebe was too smart not to have a backup plan." Said Sarah, she pushed away from the wall and sat in the chair. "She wasn't the one who healed and repaired those bodies. Like you said, she needed to focus."

Carolyn sighed impatiently.

"You're not telling us anything we don't know, Sarah."

"Yes, but did you know she's still alive?" Sarah waited a beat, as she let the bomb drop. Shocked silence met her statement.

"What the fuck are you talking about?" Jacob shouted, slamming his hands on the desk as Carolyn had done earlier. The fear, now turning to undeniable terror, as he thought of what that could mean. Sarah smiled knowingly at him.

"There are two of her, you fool." She said with relish. "She has done something that not even I could possibly fathom, and trust me, I'd seen it all."

Carolyn dragged Sarah out of the chair by her shirt and yanked her face close to hers.

"Stop speaking in riddles, bitch, I want to know."

Sarah smiled and was only too happy to oblige, if it would mean being Carolyn's number one, she would do anything.

"I had only suspected it at first. Thinking I was going crazy. But it all started coming together....Amanda."

She whispered the name like a secret.

"It was Amanda all along. She was never too far away from Phoebe. But they were always careful never to be directly next to each other in the presence of others for too long."

She looked at Jacob.

"If they stood together, you could see how their movements were almost identical. It was weird. Like watching a mirrored reflection of someone. I still wasn't sure, even then. They were very careful. So I decided to test my suspicions one night."

Sarah smiled as she sat back down in the chair, looking at Carolyn.

"Phoebe had a call to tend to a patient. I saw her leave her house. I had planned it all at the right exact time. I disguised myself that night. I met her on the street, wearing a ski mask and dressed in black. I wasn't going to kill her. I just wanted to see. I sliced her on the arm with a knife," Sarah showed them, "along her elbow, and I'd left her there. Bleeding. I wanted it to seem like an attempted assault. I left, but I didn't go home." She smiled wickedly.

"I ran to Amanda's house, and I saw her through the back window of her home. She was standing in her kitchen washing away a long jagged scar on her arm, that was disappearing even as she was cleaning it."

Jacob stared at her. His body numb.

"That doesn't mean anything."
He said, his voice was clipped.

Carolyn remained quiet, watching her.

"Perhaps not," Sarah snarled at him, "But then again, maybe it does. There's only one way to find out for sure if I'm wrong. If I am, no harm done. But If I'm right…"

"Then there's still a chance we can obtain the key." Carolyn finished for her. Her blood sang in excitement. There was still a chance.

Jacob looked at them. The wheels in his head turning fast. If Sarah was right, then his wife wasn't really dead. It was unthinkable. But possible.
Perhaps this was his only chance to correct his error.

"Okay." He said, resolved. "So what do we do now?"

Carolyn smiled at him. This was the part she loved. She spoke to them softly.

"Let's go find Amanda."

CHAPTER FIFTEEN

It felt so weird doing things this way.
Amanda sat on the edge of Vanessa's bed and stared
at her.

This was her daughter. She had to accept that now.
She had trained her mind for so long to think like a
separate person. To act, talk, and simply be different.
It was almost like a long heavy burden being lifted
from her, now that she was able to be who she truly
was. Phoebe.

"I messed up, 'nessa." She said, as she stared out
the window into the dark night.

"I was young, and alone. I wanted somebody.
Anybody. Even to the point where I convinced
myself that Amanda wasn't part of me."

Vanessa stared at Amanda solemnly; her eyes were
sad and confused. She looked at her beautiful auburn
hair. The way it always flowed down her back.
Her lovely green eyes that were so piercing and
sincere. Her soft face that was heart shaped and
sensuous. Everything about her was beautiful and
strong, courageous and loyal. Just like Phoebe.

"I don't know what to say." Vanessa said quietly.
"You're my mom, yet you're not.

You're this second identity my mother created. Almost like having multiple personalities. The only difference is she was able to make hers real."

The tears threatened to spill, but she held them back. How could she explain to Amanda that she would never be able to see her as her real mother? She just couldn't. Her heart knew she was, but her mind could not accept the different face, the hair, the voice. It wasn't mom.

Miserable, Vanessa finally let the tears flow.

Amanda's heart ripped. She had done this to her. In her desire to be like everyone else, she had hurt her daughter. Perhaps it would be easier for both of them if she just stayed as Amanda.

Perhaps Phoebe truly was dead. Taking Vanessa into her arms, she rocked her gently. Smoothing her hair and comforting her. At all costs, she needed to protect her. She was all she had now. And she couldn't forget the threat that still lurked. Her daughter was in danger.

"Sweetie," at the sound of Amanda's soft voice, Vanessa wiped her eyes, and looked at her. "There's something I still need to tell you. About who your mom really was, and the danger you are in. Something you should know." Vanessa sniffled, trying to make the pain go away.

"It's about your gift and what it can do."

Vanessa's eyes darkened.

"No. I don't want to hear any more about spells and powers. It's good for nothing! All it has done is brought pain and death!"

Amanda swallowed down the lump of fear as she stared at her. Vanessa had the same stubbornness. The same iron will. She tried again.

"Listen to me 'nessa. There's still danger. I need to tell you about your father---"

"All I ever wanted was you!!" She interrupted her, shouting and jumping from the bed. "But when I came home from school you were always too busy with your patients!"

"Vanessa that's not true!" Amanda reached for her, the tears stinging her eyes. But she evaded her.

"All I ever wanted was to have a normal life. A normal mom and dad! To be loved! Not to be a damn witch!!"

"Vanessa, you are not a witch! Please, listen to me!"

But Vanessa couldn't hear her. She was screaming at the top of her lungs. Her rage and fury was making the walls tremble, and the house shake.
Amanda saw what was happening and turned to her with real fright.

"Vanessa, you need to calm down! You need to control your anger!!"

"Don't tell me what to do! You are not my mother, and never will be!!"

She was completely out of control. A thin crack began to spread along the ceiling.

Amanda closed her eyes and focused.

A soft wind blew into the room, ruffling her daughter's hair.

As soon as Vanessa felt it, she collapsed to her knees in deep wracking sobs.

The warm breeze wrapped around her like a blanket. She felt the warmth, the protection.
She felt her mother. She looked up, her face soaked with tears.

"Mom." She whispered. Trembling.

Amanda walked over to her and opened her arms. Jumping up, Vanessa leaped into them. Feeling all of her rage and confusion melt away. There was no doubt in her mind as to who held her.

"I'm here, sweetie." Amanda whispered, as she kissed her forehead. "I've always been here."

Vanessa sighed and trembled, as she held onto her.

"I love you, mom." She said softly. "And I always will."

***

Amanda spent the night with her. She didn't trust leaving her alone with Jacob.

She still hadn't figured out how to deal with him as of yet, and she couldn't bring herself to broach the subject to Vanessa again.

But Jacob never came home that night. Vanessa got up, refreshed, and left the house early that morning.

No doubt to meet the love of her life.

Amanda had only learned of his name last night as they talked into the late hours. Vanessa planned to introduce Christopher to her later on today.

She sighed and began to prepare her things to leave. There was still much to be done. Everyone would expect Phoebe's things to be put away. Or given to Vanessa. Amanda gently caressed the desk where she had worked. Where Phoebe had worked. Disgusted, she turned away. Nothing would ever be the same again. She'd had a nightmare last night. Amanda had relived the whole thing. The burning, the sexual assault, the invasion of her soul.

The only problem with splitting the spirit, was that you tended to relive your own death. For the rest of your life.

129

Getting her things, she was deep in thought.

The town was having a meeting tonight about what to do concerning the three murders.
She intended to be there, with the evidence to put away those who she knew were responsible.

A sudden sound from behind startled her into dropping her papers.

A rough hand grabbed her, closing over her mouth. Amanda tried not to panic. Focusing her mind, her attacker was flung away from her. Crashing against the wall. One of the bookshelves broke and plummeted to the floor.

She swung around to face her assailant.

Shaking his head, Jacob stumbled to his feet. Amanda's eyes narrowed in hate.

"Jacob." She wondered how she hadn't heard him come in.

He stared at her, swiping the blood from his lip.

"So it's true." He sneered. Taking a step toward her. "It was you all along."

Amanda realized her fatal mistake too late. She hadn't meant to use her power. To reveal her long kept secret. But now that she was one again, it had come naturally, and without thought. As she struggled to figure out what to do, she felt a sharp blow from behind. Then, there was only darkness.

***

Amanda opened her eyes slowly. It was dark. It took her vision a moment to adjust.
She was in the basement of the house. Jerking her head, she saw Jacob standing to the side, watching her. A sharp pain throbbed at the back of her head. She was tied. Her wrists were in chains that were attached to the wall. She stood pinned against it, her arms were stretched out on either side of her, and her legs were imprisoned as well. Held down by shackles. Suddenly, Amanda realized that she was completely naked.

She thrashed and bucked against the chains.
"Let me go!!" She shouted at Jacob.

He smiled, enjoying the view.

"I don't think so my dear. I think I like you Just the way you are." He laughed wickedly. Amanda took a deep breath and focused her energy.

"I wouldn't do that if I were you."

A silky smooth voice said from her left. She gasped and saw Carolyn. She was standing next to her, just as naked as she was.

"If you try to use your power to free yourself, your daughter will die."

"No!!" Amanda looked at Jacob who smiled in acknowledgement.

"Right now, sweet Vanessa is being watched by someone. You make one wrong move, and the bullet will hit her before she even knows what happened."

Her body trembled with fear for Vanessa. They could not be allowed to hurt her child. Not this time.

"What do you want?" She said viciously.

"You know what we want."

Carolyn's tongue licked the side of her face. Amanda jerked away in disgust.

"It will be such a pleasure to get to taste you twice. You're probably even sweeter in this body, than you were in Phoebe's."

She glided a hand down Amanda's stomach.

"Give us the key, and we won't harm Vanessa." Said Jacob.

"We know you're not stupid to fall for the same trick twice. I know you're stronger. You won't allow yourself to lose focus like you did before." He smiled cruelly. "However, there is more than one way to kill a witch."

"Go to hell!" Amanda shouted at him. "I don't have the key! You know I can't help you!"

Carolyn's hands cupped her round breasts and squeezed painfully.

"We shall see." She whispered.

Suddenly, Amanda saw candles light up all around the room. She now could see everything. Blood streaked the walls. Two dead animals lay on either side of her. Their blood seeping into a pool at her feet.

"You sick fuck!!" She screamed at them. Thrashing against her chains. She didn't know what to do. If she used her gift, Vanessa would die. If she didn't, so would she.

"Give it to me, Amanda." Carolyn's eyes blazed red, and her flaming hair blew around her.

Amanda could see the demon in her. The house started to rattle as they began the ritual.
Jacob began to chant, kneeling before the animals and dipping his hands into their blood. His clothes ripped away from his body. She could see the claws sticking out of his back.

 Carolyn picked up a whip. It was long and black, with sharp pointy nails. She reared back her hand and struck her with it. Her blood spilling to the floor, mingling with the animals'.

Grabbing her face, she smiled viciously as she felt
Amanda tremble.

"Do you enjoy the pain, my dear?" She whispered,
her tongue licking all over her face.
"Because I certainly enjoy giving it."

Dropping the whip, Carolyn began her sexual assault
on her weak and bleeding body.
Amanda refused to scream again. The pain and
torture were unthinkable.

To be going through all of this again. She wasn't
going to let it happen. She felt the rage begin to build.
Something inside her was beginning to crack.

"Yes!" Jacob shouted. His eyes wildly crazed. The
basement floor began to crack open, and a dark red
glow seeped from below.

Carolyn continued to rub herself against Amanda.
Touching, sucking, biting, devouring.

"Yes." She crooned, as Amanda's head craned back
in fury. "Give it to me. Give it all to me!!"

"No!!" Amanda cried out in torment.

The darkness was nearly free. Her body was on fire.
Tormented with sexual pleasure and pain. The ground
opened wider, and a low, deep endless moan could be
heard from the very depths. As Amanda prepared to
release what was inside of her, she thought of
Vanessa.

"I can't." She whispered, the tears falling from her eyes. She refused to let it happen. "No, you will not succeed!!" The chains tore away from her body, and Carolyn was flung across the room.

"You're too late!!" Jacob cried.

The horns were protruding from his head, and his eyes were blazing.

"Look and behold!!"

Amanda watched in slow dawning terror, as the ground opened wider. The house shook, and hot flames began to rise from below. With a sinking realization, she knew that if she didn't close it, if what was in that ground was allowed to come up, nothing could stop it once it arrived.
She could not let it escape.

"Vanessa," She whispered, closing her eyes, "I love you."

Before they could stop her, Amanda leaped into the air, and jumped headfirst into the raging flames.

"Nooo!!!!!" Jacob screamed, running after her. But he was too late.

An inhuman roar erupted from below and screeched in agony. Blood spewed up from within the gaping floor and showered the basement. The ground trembled, and slowly closed shut. The blood and screams vanished as if they were never there.

Jacob looked up. His horns had disappeared, and his clothes were back in place.

Amanda was gone.

His cries of failure and defeat reached the top of the woods a distance away.

Not farther than that, Vanessa jerked away from Christopher, as a deep spasm shook her body. She fell on her face into the grass and wept.

 "Damn you!"
She shouted in torment.
"Damn you!!"

   Christopher was shoved away as he tried to touch her, not understanding what was wrong with her. But she didn't want his touch.

No one could help her now. She knew now, that she was utterly alone.

CHAPTER SIXTEEN

One Year Later

Mrs. Basely unlocked her shop and slowly walked in. Switching on the lights, she went around the counter to begin her morning routine of checking inventory and setting up the register for the day's sales. Her shoulders were slouched and weary. Her bones made a dull cracking sound whenever she moved. Her arthritis was getting worse. Each day, it became harder and harder to come to work. It was so painful to move.

Her mouth was set in a grim, permanent line of hostility. Over the past year, she'd been unapproachable, mean and surly. Almost no one came into her store these days. Actually preferring to drive miles away from town, to the nearest supermarket. It was driving her into debt. With a grimace, she painfully walked over to her stocks and supplies, and began to take count. Writing on her clipboard. Tears of pain and frustration began to sting her eyes as she slowly forced her fingers to move with the pen.

Nothing had been the same since Phoebe and Amanda had died last year. Most of the people had moved away, but there was still a good bit that chose to stay. The state had finally taken notice of the murders and tragedies going on in Melrose. After four people had already died.

137

There'd been an investigation that was still open. Still unsolved to this day. There was really no one to lend any proof or suspects. The mysterious disappearance of Phoebe's remaining group members, Crystal White and Barbara Maple, remained an open case as well. There had been no trace of them. No indication that they'd left town, or if they were still alive.

They'd simply vanished.

Mrs. Basely's grimace turned into a snarl. Putting one foot in front of the other, she began to move down the aisle. Forcing herself to bear the pain. Sweat trickled down her face, and her frail body trembled. Without Phoebe or Amanda, her body had slowly gone into disrepair. Shutting down limb by limb. She would never admit it. Not even to herself. But she was dying.

With each passing day, the inevitable drew closer. The hostility hid her pain and torment like a thick blanket. Allowing the ice to freeze whatever hurt she may have felt, when the last of her hope died with Amanda. Sweet, lovely Amanda. So very much like Phoebe. It had been easy to love her. To pretend she was her daughter. A small stab of pain pierced through the ice she had built around her heart. Mrs. Basely paused, as she felt the tremor flow through her.

Leaning her hand on the food stands, she took a deep breath.

No. She thought to herself. She would not give in. All hope had not died with Phoebe and Amanda. Straightening herself, she stubbornly ignored the pain, and resumed counting.

The demons thought they had won.

Moving into the bread aisle, her eyes narrowed. She was an old woman, and her time was nearly up. Her hair was completely white, wrapped tightly into a bun at her nape. The dull gray flowered dress she wore hung on her long bony frame.

Her glasses were always slipping off of her haggard face. Within one year, it felt as if she'd aged twenty times her sixty-seven years. Her face was now drawn and limp. The skin now hung on her body where she used to have healthy, strong flesh and bones. Now, death was calling her. But she stubbornly refused to go.

"Not yet." She mumbled, moving through another aisle. "I still have work to do."

Mrs. Basely's hands shook as she tried to hold the clipboard steady. She'd had another nightmare last night. It wasn't one of her usual. Where she dreamed of her husband, Clifford Basely, driving out to the McMann ranch for their monthly supplies, and losing control of the car. He'd had a head on collision with another driver. Someone from out of town. That was over ten years ago.

She'd long since buried her Cliff and accepted the fact that she had never been meant to have children. She'd put away her long ago dreams of family and happiness. The ones that she and Cliff had high hopes for, when they'd first moved to Melrose. The nightmare of his death always came every now and then. She would awaken in a pool of sweat, crying out for her Cliff.

But the nightmare she'd had last night, had nothing to do with Clifford Basely.

Her breath began to quicken, as the memory of the darkness and complete emptiness she'd felt last night, returned to her in full force.

Phoebe and Amanda had been standing side by side holding hands. Looking at her. She had reached out for them, when suddenly, their image shifted and blurred. She watched as Phoebe and Amanda merged into one. One woman. Not two.

Mrs. Basely understood then and began to sob.

Phoebe had smiled at her, and then looked to her side. Vanessa was standing next to her. Beautiful and happy. But there was something forming over her head. Some sort of dark cloud or mist. Both Phoebe and Vanessa were completely unaware of the danger. Mrs. Basely screamed and shouted, trying to warn them. But it was no use. The dark cloud surrounded Vanessa, snatching her away from Phoebe.

Phoebe screamed, but no sound could be heard from her mouth. Vanessa was lifted off her feet, spinning in the air, entrapped in the dark mist. Her mouth wide open in a silent scream. And then the mist had cut her in half. Splitting her body open, and she exploded into millions of pieces.

Mrs. Basely clutched her chest, as a sharp pain gripped her. Red dots formed before her eyes, and she was forced to her knees, gasping and trembling. She was out of time. She needed to do it now. Bracing herself on the shelves, she used the last bit of her strength to hoist herself up.

Panting heavily, Mrs. Basely slowly trudged to the back of the store where her office was. There was still hope. And all hope rested on her. She went to the desk and withdrew a key that hung on a string from around her neck. Unlocking the drawer, she opened it and withdrew a large journal. It was old and dusty. She hadn't touched it since Maryanne had given it to her twenty seven years ago. Maryanne O'Connor. Phoebe's mother. She stood for a long while, simply staring at it. Maryanne had given it to her the very day before she died.

"Keep it safe for me, Mrs. Basely." She shoved it into her hands; a sad look of regret was in her eyes. Her long black hair was flowing around her shoulders. Her beautiful young face was strained and filled with pain.

"What's wrong with you child? What am I supposed to do with this book? What is it?"

Mrs. Basely had fired the questions at her in worry and confusion.

"You'll know when the time comes." Maryanne whispered. A tear falling from her eye.

"She is the only one who can redeem us."

She'd run away without another word to her, disappearing into the dark night. By the very next day, she was dead. Died in a tragic accident.

Mrs. Basely had put the journal away, intending to give it to Phoebe. But she'd never felt compelled to do so. As she stared at the dusty large book, she now knew the meaning of those painfully spoken words, that late night so many years ago. She'd never opened it. Never heeded her curiosity.

It was not for her eyes, but for the one Maryanne had said would redeem them. Gathering the book into her arms, she slowly left the office. Her tired, weary body, rasping out weak spurts of breath. There was one last thing she needed to do before she gave in to the call of death.

***

Christopher knocked on the hardwood door for the tenth time. Clenching his jaw in frustration, he looked up at the middle second story window that belonged to Vanessa.

What was going on? He wondered, irritated.

He'd told her he was coming by to see her today. When they'd spoken on the phone last night, she'd seemed distracted. Even edgy. She hadn't been acting like herself lately. Then again, Vanessa hadn't been the same since her mom and aunt had died last year. He sighed deeply and ran a hand roughly through his hair.

He thought he might've been able to help her. To ease some of her pain, by asking her to marry him. However, since her aunt's death had followed almost right after her mom's, he knew wedding bells were the furthest things from her mind. The last time he'd seen her had been three days ago. For Christopher, who was used to seeing the girl he loved every day, that was too long. She'd changed in more ways than one, and he was afraid he was losing her.

Shoving his hands into his pockets, Christopher turned away and started down the steps. Pulling his jacket closer around him. He noticed the flowers around the house had long died and the grass had never been cut. All of the effort that Vanessa's mom had put into caring for the garden had gone to waste, even before the season had changed.

The brisk October wind whipped through his hair as he started to walk away. Suddenly, the door opened up behind him. Turning, he saw Vanessa's father, Jacob Dickens, standing in the doorway. His cold eyes pinning him, almost paralyzed him to the spot.

Pretending he was unaffected by Mr. Dickens intimidating presence, he walked back towards him.

143

They'd never really had the opportunity of meeting face to face, and Vanessa never made any attempt to introduce him.

"Mr. Dickens, I apologize for showing up like this. I'm afraid we've never had the pleasure of meeting. I'm Christopher McMann, a friend of Vanessa's."

He extended his hand. Jacob's eyes never left his. Remaining still as a statue, he made no move to shake his hand, or even acknowledge a word he'd said. He simply stared at him. Christopher felt the coldness crawl up his back.

The look in his eyes could only be described as lethal. Like a man who was one second away from killing an enemy, and feasting on his bones. Christopher swallowed and lowered his hand, taking a step back.

This seemed to please Jacob. Immensely.

"I know who you are."

His voice was smooth. Charming. The perfect businessman. Christopher wondered, looking at him, if he'd ever had a wrinkle mar his perfect suit. Jacob's eyes suddenly seemed to glint with anticipation.

"Please, won't you come in?"

CHAPTER SEVENTEEN

Christopher came into the house and took a look around. He'd only been inside one time, almost a year ago, when he and Vanessa had first started dating. The house looked nothing like he remembered it. The long row of bookshelves that had lined the living room walls were completely gone.

Phoebe's beautiful brown desk that had stood at the side of the room, was nowhere to be seen. The lovely white flowered drapes that had hung cheerfully on the windows were gone. Replaced by dark brown ones, almost devoid of any color at all. They successfully blocked out any light from outside. The creamy beige sofa and loveseat was now black leather, with a black shiny coffee table in between. There were no end tables, no flowers, no pictures of any kind that graced the walls. The room was bare, other than the sofa, loveseat and table. The soft comfortable brown carpet was gone. There was only gleaming hardwood floor.

Christopher's stricken gaze searched the room. There was not a speck of dust anywhere. Even the sofa seemed to shine. There was now a chandelier that hung in the room, sparkling with brilliance. The house had the feel of cold perfection. Empty, and physically without blemish. Like its owner.

Shaken down to the core, Christopher walked over to the sofa and prepared to sit down.

A cold steely hand gripped his shoulder painfully.

"We do not sit on the furniture, in this house."

Jacob's voice held a note of warning in it, edged with hostility and malice. Christopher was truly frightened now.

"Uh, I'm sorry sir, I didn't know. I apologize."

Jacob's eyes shone for an instant with an unholy light, then he released him, walking around the room.

"What can I do for you, Mr. McMann?" He drawled the name like it was a bad taste in his mouth. Christopher's heart was still racing.

"Actually, I just came to speak with Vanessa. I had told her I would be dropping by. Is she home?"

Jacob's back was turned to him. He did not see his eyes glow red hot. Or the horns that threatened to rise out of his head. With effort, he regained control.

"She is not here." Jacob said, turning back towards him and smiling slowly. He would like nothing more than to rip his pathetic body in two. But he could not. His death was not part of his master's plan. At least not now.

"How well do you know my daughter, Mr. McMann?" He asked him, disappearing into the kitchen and retuning with a tall wine glass, filled with a dark red liquid. He did not offer his guest a drink.

"Well I uh…we've been friends for about a year now. She goes to the school out of town—"

"You are well over the age of eighteen, Mr. McMann. And you do not attend school. So I repeat, how well do you know my daughter?"

Christopher's heart thudded against his chest. The sweat trickled down his brow. He didn't know what it was about this man that frightened him so much. His own father, who was much tougher and louder, could not even make him flinch. But there was something about Jacob Dickens that made his skin crawl.

"Well, we met last year in Mrs. Green's supply goods store. We've grown very close."

Thinking of Vanessa, Christopher straightened up and choked down the fear.

"I might as well tell you that I plan to marry her. I would like for her to be my wife. It would give me great satisfaction, and no doubt please Vanessa, if we were to have your blessing."

Jacob felt the hate rip inside of him. The burning hunger threatened to overtake him at Christopher's words.

"Excuse me a moment."

He shoved past Christopher and went into the kitchen. He took the bottle out of the cabinet and drank hungrily.

The torment easing, his horns receding into his head. Taking a deep breath, a cruel evil smile spread across his face. Coming back into the living room, Jacob eyed Christopher. He was such an idealistic fool. Breaking his spirit was going to be fun.

"Did you know Mr. McMann, that my daughter is the child of a witch?"

He said the words pleasantly, as if they were old friends. The familiar anger began to root itself in Christopher's body. He was tired of the lies, and the taunts from the ranch hands and other people, about Vanessa.

"I don't believe in witches, sir. And I can't believe you would say such a thing about your wife." He tried to control his outrage.

Jacob reared back his head and laughed. It was cold and wicked.

"Then you have answered my question after all, young fool. You do not know my daughter."

Christopher's muscles tensed, ready to pounce.

"How dare you---" he started, but Jacob cut him off. The venom in his eyes was enough to make him think twice.

"You know nothing about her!" Jacob sneered. "She uses you, and tells you lies. Using the same lies and deceit that her mother used on me. She does not love you, and never has."

Christopher's eyes narrowed with anger, and he balled his fists.

"I wish I had known the type of man you are. I would've taken Vanessa away from here a long time ago."

He turned to leave, striding angrily to the door.

"You think you're the only one." Jacob's sinister voice stopped him. "The only one to have her, be with her. Ask her for yourself, you pathetic fool. And you will find that you're not the only one who has sampled her treasures."

In wild rage, Christopher turned and leaped at Jacob. But he was gone. His laughter echoing through the walls. In panicked dismay, he turned and ran out of the house. The laughter followed him.

Christopher never saw Vanessa's pale and tear streaked face in the window, her hands on the glass. Her eyes were a silent cry for help.

***

Christopher ran all the way home, panting and wheezing. The rage that he felt was still with him. He needed to blow off some steam. Going to the stables, he entered and walked purposely toward Dominance, his black stallion. Flying on his back in one leap, he and Dominance charged out of the stables. People jumped out of the way, as horse and rider raced through the fields.

The familiar freedom and power began to overtake him, and soon the anger subsided. He began to think about the last few months. Within the past year, Vanessa had been distant. Almost never really wanting to touch. They hadn't made love in almost a year.

As Christopher led Dominance to a trot, he reined him in at their favorite spot. The field of violets. Right now, it was nothing but a tall field of brown grass. That would, come next spring, sprout into lovely violets again.

The memory came to him with bitter sweetness. The days and nights spent making love. The sighs of pleasure. The happy whispers, the plans to be together forever.

His shoulders slumped; he sat down and leaned against a tree. Their initials were carved in it, with a big heart and arrow going through it. Was it possible she didn't love him anymore? Was there even a small chance that what her father had said was true?

His jaw clenched as he thought of Jacob Dickens. There was something truly wrong with that man. The whole town had something truly wrong with it. Four murders and two disappearances. And no one had a clue as to what was going on. Not the state police or even the townspeople. Some had moved away, others stayed away. Melrose was now a place nobody really wanted to go near. They feared something awful was going on over there. Perhaps they were right. He sighed.

Next year, he would be leaving for Greenville, North Carolina, to take over the main ranch there. He'd hoped to be leaving as a married man. Now he wasn't so sure anymore. He feared that Vanessa no longer wanted to see him. He didn't know why she was avoiding him, but it made him more and more confused.

"Chris!!" He heard his father calling his name. Getting up, he jumped back on Dominance and galloped towards the house. When he reached the ranch, his father walked up to him. "You've got a visitor!" He barked. "You should never keep a lady waiting!"

He turned and stalked away.

Swift pleasure poured through his body at his father's words. Vanessa had come to see him.

Jumping off his horse, he gave Dominance over to one of the ranch hands, and ran into the house. He

151

stopped cold when he noticed the beautiful blond, sitting in the armchair in the parlor. Her long legs were crossed.

She wore tight blue faded jeans that hugged her every curve, and a white t-shirt tucked within it. Her body was slim and toned, and her hair was waves of silk and loveliness. Her eyes were a soft blue and were bright with amusement. She rose gracefully from the chair.

"Hello, Christopher." Her voice was light and easy. It's a pleasure to finally see you again."

She extended her soft lovely hand. He shook it, still shocked and confused.

It was Sophia Roberts, A woman he had met in passing almost two years ago.

"I'm sorry, but I wasn't expecting company." He began, unsure of himself.

"Oh, it's okay." Sophia said, smiling pleasantly. It was like a bright morning sun. "I just wanted to stop by. I'm your new neighbor. I just bought the Hillerson farm."

Christopher felt genuine surprise, and a small spark of pleasure, at having such a lovely neighbor. If his heart was not already taken, he might've enjoyed the pleasure of getting to know her all over again.

***

Outside the house, Robert McMann smiled secretly to himself as he walked to the sheds. The new owner of the Hillerson farm was a pretty little thing, and perfect for his son. Hopefully, Sophia could take his son as far away from that witch's nest as possible.

And far away from that girl.

CHAPTER EIGHTEEN

Vanessa no longer attended school.

After her mom and Amanda died, her father had told her there was no point in going to school. He did not believe in women being taught anything. Except to clean. He had completely changed.

Vanessa sat on a rock in the woods. She threw small pebbles into a little pond. Her beautiful face was sad and drawn. She never bothered to smile anymore. What was the point? The cold wind rustled the trees around her. Her hair was tied tightly into a bun at her nape. Just as her mother used to wear it. She never wore it loose anymore. The only one who used to love to see it that way, no longer wanted any part of her.

No tears came to her eyes, as the dull ache slashed through her heart.

Christopher, the love of her life, her only reason to go on, no longer loved her. Vanessa stared at the letter in her hand that she'd brought along with her. The letter Christopher had written to her. Telling her what he thought of her. How he never wanted to see her again.

The pain threatened to choke her as she stood up, numb from the cold. Her boots crunched over dirt;

her hands trembled. The choking feeling became overbearing.

She ran over to the pond and retched. Her body heaving and jerking until the spasms subsided. Falling to the ground, weak and broken, she still could not cry the tears that begged for release.

She'd needed time. She wanted to tell him. Wanted to go to him and tell him why she'd been so distant. Why she didn't know herself anymore. But she couldn't.

She didn't know how to tell him the truth. She was afraid he'd recoil from her. Afraid he would turn his love away. In the end, it had happened anyway.

Vanessa glanced at the letter lying on the floor. He sounded so angry. She sat up, taking the paper and putting it back in her pocket. She remembered every line. Every hateful word.

"I'm tired of the lies, and I'm tired of you. I know what you are. It's over. I don't ever want to see or hear from you again." It was signed in his loving script, Christopher.

Shakily, Vanessa got to her feet and began to walk through the woods. The place no longer held any fear for her. She was completely numb. The dizziness made her stumble.

Her father told her what he said. The day he'd come to see her, over a week ago.

"He just came to give you this." Jacob gave her the letter, sealed in a crisp white envelope.

"I tried to convince him to stay, to at least see you. But he refused. He left angry and said he would have nothing to do with a witch's daughter."

Vanessa had intended to run after him, but her father stopped her with a cold hand.

"What are the rules of this house?" He asked her. Vanessa trembled and shrunk away. She had paid dearly for breaking the rules last time.
She thought of her dog's mangled body, and the ache intensified.

Holding the letter in her hand, she had climbed dejectedly back up the stairs to her room. She must not disobey the rules of the house. This meant she could not leave as long as her father was home from work. She was to remain inside at all times. Always obedient. Always submissive.

Vanessa walked slowly through the woods; a vacant emptiness swam within the depths of her eyes. She'd seen Christopher run from the house that day. As if he couldn't wait to get away. She had been sleeping. Twisting and turning in the midst of a nightmare. She was awakened by loud shouting, and the sound of running feet. Hurrying to the window, Vanessa was just in time to see Christopher race away, as if hounds from hell chased him.

He left her alone just as everyone else did. Everyone except her father. When she tried to call his house a few days later, his father answered. He told her in a clipped voice that Christopher was busy. Sometimes the phone just rang. Over the past week, she'd even tried sending letters. Praying he would come to her. That he would take her in his arms and love her the way he used to. Now, it was too late.

The cold wind whistled around her, turning her cheeks a dull blue. She'd only worn a thick knitted dark blue sweater and jeans. She was oblivious to the weather. She could not feel the coldness of her skin, because her insides were numb with frost.

***

Vanessa arrived home late. She'd lost track of time and now, she was truly afraid. Running around back, she quickly took off her boots and came in through the back door. Hurrying, she tiptoed up the stairs in her socks. Hoping. Praying. Her body was trembling with fear. Glancing behind her, she darted her eyes in every direction. Watching.

Slowly, she backed up into her room and closed the door quietly.

"Who are you hiding from, Vanessa?"

The voice slammed into the very heart of her terror. Whirling around in fright, she shook violently as she backed up into the door.

157

"N..n..no one, father. I was just making sure I didn't disturb your sleep."

"You know I do not sleep at night."

Jacob was laying on her bed. His legs were crossed at the ankles, and his head was cushioned into her soft pillows. He loved the way they smelled of her hair and body.

"Y…yes, father. Forgive me, father."

Her eyes were wide balls of fear. Jacob loved it, as he watched her. He loved to see his precious daughter cowering before him.

"Did you go to that boy?" He got up from the bed in one smooth motion, and advanced on her slowly.

"No! No father please! I did not disobey you!" Vanessa's eyes now released the tears she'd been holding back for so long.

"Please..daddy." She begged him. "No more. Please."

His hand whipped out and cracked against her soft cheek. She spun across the room and crashed into her dresser. She whimpered and fell to her knees in pain. She did not need to hear him say it. She knew the rules of the house.

Trembling, her tears dried up as she slowly lifted her sweater over her head.

Her bra followed. Then her pants, socks and underwear. Naked, Vanessa knelt down and crawled over to Jacob on all fours. Keeping her head down. She reached his feet, and gently touching his shoes, kissed each of them.

"I'm sorry father." She said softly. Her voice shaking. "I will not disobey you again."

Jacob smiled as the sweet pleasure began to course through his body.

"That's my little girl." He said softly. Vanessa got up and stood before him. Her body trembling, but her face was still. Emotionless.

Jacob slowly began to undress. The horns stretched from his head. His eyes were red holes of flames, and his body bled from numerous cuts and gashes, and the claws that stuck from his back. Her body shuddered.

Screeching a demonic cry, Jacob grabbed Vanessa by the hair and threw her onto the bed.
She cried out in pain, as she hit the headboard. Tuning quickly, she forced herself not to feel, to will away the pain, as her father approached her.

She knew what he would do if she tried to run. His claw like feet clicked on the hardwood floor as he came closer. Rasping, Jacob climbed onto the bed and moved on top of her. Vanessa held herself still, and squeezed her eyes shut. The pain began.
She could not help it. She screamed.

Jacob growled and emitted a liquid fiery substance into her open mouth. Bucking and convulsing, Vanessa's body twitched, as the liquid shot down her throat. Her eyes rolled into the back of her head. He closed his mouth, and the invasion ceased. He continued to plunge into her.

She knew sometimes, it could take hours. Jacob looked into her eyes as he used her body, and viciously grabbed her face.

"Look at me!!" He screeched. His voice was deep and distorted. "You are mine, and mine alone!! No one else can ever have you! Especially that pathetic boy!!" He rammed harder into her than usual. Vanessa felt her flesh begin to rip.

"How dare he come here thinking he could possibly have you?! No one can take what is mine!!" His voice was that of a monstrous animal from the very depths of hell. As he tore into her very soul, something reached her as eternal darkness began to take hold of her.

Something Jacob had said.

He'd lied to her, a tiny voice she thought long dead, whispered to her. The voice of anger.

Jacob continued to batter her body until he was spent. He glanced down at her. A look of triumph on his face. Vanessa remained still as a statue, as he climbed off of her. His words swimming through her head. Reaching deep down inside of her to pull out a small bit of emotion. Hope. Christopher had not abandoned her. He had come looking for her. Wanting her. He still loved her. It had all been a cruel and dark lie.

She looked at her father as his body began to change back. His cool, evil composure back in place. He looked at her impassively, as he made to leave the room.

"I will expect my dinner in ten minutes, or next time, the pain will be worse." He turned and left the room. Vanessa stared at the closed door.

Her bloody, beaten body still and cold on the bed. A low glimmer of light began to burn in her eyes.

"No, father." She whispered into the silent room. "Soon my pain will end. But yours will last for all eternity." Closing her eyes, her body began to heal itself.

The way it always had since she was a little girl. She looked toward the window.

Feeling hope and love burning brighter inside of her. Taking away her torment.

She would see Christopher again. And if hope could hear her, he would love her despite the evil, and rescue her. She sighed, Ready.
Waiting for the dawn.
Soon, Christopher would know the truth.

CHAPTER NINETEEN

Christopher finished up his work for the day. Tired and weary, he rode Dominance back home. The past weeks had been rough. He had tried to put Vanessa out of his mind. Tried to accept the fact that she no longer loved him. But he couldn't.

His father constantly berated him for neglecting the opportunity to snatch up a beautiful woman like Sophia. Everyone on the ranch steered clear of him. His anger and turmoil seemed to affect everything around him.

Perhaps it was time to give her up. His heart wrenched at the thought, and he lowered his head.

From somewhere far away, he could hear his name being called. He ignored it, preferring to be alone. But whoever it was persisted. Christopher raised his head, annoyed. Suddenly, he realized the direction of the voice. It was coming from behind him. Back where the pastures and fields were. Not the ranch. Swinging Dominance around, he galloped towards the open fields, the cold wind whipping through his hair.

He saw her standing there. Her hair was blowing wildly about her face. Christopher raced his horse faster. Charging up to her, Vanessa's eyes widened as he swept her from the ground. He lifted her onto Dominance and placed her in front of him. She laughed joyfully when his strong arms came around her. Christopher kissed her gently on the neck and face, her lips and shoulders. He simply could not get enough of her. And neither could she.

"I missed you." Christopher said roughly. He breathed in her scent and let it fill his nostrils, taking her hair and kissing it lovingly.

"And I've missed you, my love. I missed you so much." Vanessa said softly. She thought her heart would burst. They rode in silence, their arms wrapped around each other in comfort and warmth. All of the doubts of the past weeks, even months, now all seemed like a long forgotten nightmare. She was here in his arms, and she still loved him. He'd been foolish to think otherwise.

He led them to the stables. Jumping off Dominance, he gently eased Vanessa into his arms and carried her up a ladder, leading to their over head secret lover's nest. The hayloft was a small area. Very rarely was it used, until Christopher had led her here one stormy night. Here, he'd shown her all of the beautiful and passionate ways to be loved.

He'd awakened something deep within her and left her soaring. Never to be the same again. Vanessa's eyes lit with pleasure when she realized where he'd taken her.

Gently, Christopher lowered her onto the hay, far back where no one could see them.
This was their secret place. Her heart pounded in anticipation. It had been so long since she'd felt his

163

touch. She wanted him to wash away her sorrow and pain, all of the ugliness.

To make her feel whole again.

He began to caress her face. Tracing the line of her jaw, the curve of her cheek. Gently closing her eyes, he tenderly kissed her lids, her forehead, and slowly went down her face. Leaving no part uncovered. Vanessa sighed, opening her arms to enfold him. There were no words.

As their lips met, she felt a fire pool within the pit of her stomach, and travel down to rest between her legs. Moaning softly, she opened her mouth and felt Christopher's tongue scorch her. Stoking the embers within her. Teasing her. He nipped her bottom lip gently, and deepened the kiss. Her body began to burn. There was a fire in her. And now, because of him, she knew exactly why she burned. He opened her mind and soul and filled her so completely; she was on the edge of bursting.

"Christopher," She whispered his name, as her body ached. He wanted to possess every part of her. To bask in her scent and her passion.

Growling low in his throat, he felt a strange sensation for the first time since he'd met her. A stirring. Almost like a deep far away call that he couldn't quite decipher. Lowering his head, he took her straining nipple into his mouth. Suckling it through her shirt. Molding her round breast with his hand.

164

Vanessa cried out his name, her body jerking in reaction.

Christopher's need seemed to overwhelm him. He felt as if he was free falling off of a cliff.
Impatient, he ripped the shirt from her body, and threw it across the loft.

Vanessa's eyes widened in shock and pleasure, as she stared up at him.

"Christopher?" Her voice held confusion in it. She'd never seen him this way before.

Not saying a word, he latched onto her nipple again, this time nipping and biting. Squeezing her breasts with a roughness and vigor he'd never shown before. Vanessa cried out in pain, completely taken off guard. She tried to push him away from her, the image of her father beginning to invade her mind.

His hands were scratching her, and she felt little strings of blood from where he bit her.

"Christopher! Stop!!" Vanessa tried slapping him, but he was impervious to her discomfort. His hands held her down possessively, while he ripped her pants from her body in one clean swipe.

"Christopher, what are you doing?!!" She fought him with all of her strength, the tears streaking her cheeks, but it was useless.

Watching in horror as the man she loved seemed to lose his mind.

Christopher ripped his clothes off in a wild frenzy, his body dripping with sweat.

He panted heavily. His muscles taught with tension and lust. His eyes began to glow with fire.

"No!!!" Vanessa shook her head back and forth, screaming with wildness, as she realized what she was seeing.

"Not you, Christopher! Not you!!" She shouted in denial, against the evidence in front of her.

A raging fire erupted within her and spread throughout her body.

The air began to crackle and sizzle.

Christopher bared his teeth and plunged deep within her. Vanessa cried out in pain, even as unbidden pleasure began to course through her. Writhing and scratching, her body bucked and arched as he plunged and rammed repeatedly in her.
The sky darkened, and thunder rumbled.
The horses reared and slammed their hooves against the stalls.

Lightening crashed through the roof of the stable and struck the ground.

Vanessa was out of control with passion, her hair flying all over the place, as Christopher drove within her relentlessly. Her body took over, and a primeval lust ruled.

His fingers dug into her flesh, gripping her round buttocks. Driving her hips into him deeper and deeper.

His eyes were bright red, claws lengthened from his hands, and his teeth grew long and pointy. Vanessa's own eyes began to glow, white hot like blazing lightening, they sizzled and scorched. Her body began to pulse with a bright shimmering heat.

"Yes!!" Vanessa cried out in joy and pleasure, as she felt wings begin to sprout from her back. Large Beautiful white silky feathered wings. They spread wide, blinding in their brilliance and beauty. She was like a butterfly that had emerged from the cocoon. Her body began to jerk as she climaxed violently. Christopher's eyes blazed with fire.

His own body coming into its own.

"You're mine!" He rasped. "All mine!!"

Gripping her tightly, he bared his sharp teeth and sank them deep within the softness of her neck. Their blood began to join. Now, Vanessa's cries of joy turned to pain, as her white wings began to change color.

Turning into a midnight black.

167

Vanessa reared back with the force of the orgasm that hit her. Completely overtaking her. Her body jumping and jerking with the spasms.

Her blackened wings began to bleed blood red, as Christopher rammed the last of himself into her raging body.

Together they screamed in torment.
Their mating ritual was completed.
They were now joined in ways far deeper than they could ever imagine.

Somewhere in the back of her mind, Vanessa knew she was damned.

CHAPTER TWENTY

Vanessa lay spent in Christopher's arms. Content to stay that way for the rest of the day.

They were both still naked. Hidden in their secret loft. Sweat covered them from head to toe, and their heart beat still pounded in their chest.

She sighed and snuggled closer. Trying to regain her breath.

She couldn't really recall everything that happened between them; all she knew was that the way they'd made love had been phenomenal.

She had never felt anything like it in her life!

Vanessa frowned as something poked at the edges of her memory. Something had happened while they'd made love. Violence. A burning. A feeling of birth, and utter despair.

And…. glowing eyes.

Her frown deepened as she tried to remember, but the images faded away. As if sensing her discomfort, Christopher gathered her closer to him.

"How do you feel?" He asked, gently kissing her moist brow.

He stroked her curved, rounded hip. Vanessa dismissed her thoughts and turned to kiss him slowly, lingering on his sweet lips.

"I feel wonderful, now that I have you."

Christopher stroked her gently. Easing her around to face him, he looked deep into her eyes. He didn't really remember what happened between them either. There was no evidence on either of them that spoke of the violence, or anything abnormal.

All he could recall was burying himself so deep within her that he'd shattered. There was a part of him that craved something…more.

As a flicker of unease spread through him, Christopher frowned and tried to remember. But he couldn't. All he knew was a feeling of bliss and a deep hunger that only Vanessa was able to fulfill. He chased his thoughts away, as he took her face in his hands and caressed her cheeks. It was high time that they talked.

"Vanessa, there's something I've been wanting to discuss with you for a while now. But I've never really been able to get around to it."

She smiled at him as he spoke. Love for him poured out of her in droves.

Christopher sighed. He was so nervous. What if she rejected him? What would he do if Vanessa didn't want to be his wife? His heart lurched at the thought. He didn't want to think about that. He couldn't.

"You know how much I love you." He began. "This past year, I know you've been through some terrible pain. And though I want to erase every tear and every heartache from your life, I know I can't."

His eyes held a world of love and warmth as he caressed her face.

"But what I can do, is bring you love, a new life filled with joy. So much, that it outweighs the pain."

He took her hands gently in his.

"Vanessa, I want to give you laughter, and happiness. I want to make love to you until the sun comes up. I want to give you children, and see your light shining in their eyes. I want you, my sweet Vanessa. Marry me. Be my wife. Share my life with me."

Christopher paused. Holding his breath as he waited for her answer.

Vanessa's eyes began to fill with water. The tears spilling over and falling onto their joined hands. Her heart pounded so fast, she thought it would bust. Here was the happiness she'd always wanted. Always longed for. Her dream had finally come true.

"Yes!!" She threw herself into his arms, laughing with happiness. Sobbing tears of joy. "Of course, I will! I love you, Christopher. I love you so much!"

"And I love you, my beautiful Vanessa."

They hugged and kissed and made slow love this time. With no fevered hunger or impatient desires. There was only love. Blooming and brightening everything within them. It was all they needed.

***

Hours later, as darkness fell upon the land, Christopher grudgingly realized he should be getting Vanessa home. Both their parents were probably worried about them. Plus, his stomach growled loudly, reminding him he'd missed supper.

"C'mon, Vanessa." He said soothingly, waking her up to get dressed. "It's late. I'd better take you home. Your father is probably worried sick."

Vanessa was slowly awakening. Stretching her beautiful body like a cat. At the mention of her father, she froze. Panic and terror lancing through her like a whiplash. Oh no. She thought with despair. Coldness took place of her sweet contentment.

Her father. She'd forgotten all about him. Oh God. How could she forget? How could she not remember the absolute horror of the cold truth?

"Vanessa? What's wrong?" Christopher saw the stark terror in her eyes, as she began to dress hurriedly. As if she feared something. Or someone.

"Nothing!" She jumped away from him. Not wanting him to touch her. How could she do this to him? How could she not tell him? The tears stung her eyes, as she felt the pain and sadness return. He'd asked her to marry him. How could she do that without telling him about her father? Christopher grabbed her arm as she tried to turn away. She was trembling violently.

"Vanessa! Tell me what's wrong! Why are you so frightened? Was it something I did? Please, Tell me!"

He couldn't stand to see her like this. If only she would tell him what was bothering her, he would make it right. He would do anything for her.
She heard the helplessness in his voice and couldn't bear it. She couldn't hurt him. He had to know the truth. He loved her, and she loved him.

They would find a way to overcome this. Vanessa turned to him. Her eyes locking with his in love and understanding.

"There are a lot of things about me I think you should know before we're married, Christopher." She began. Her voice hitching on the word, 'married.'

"I don't care about your past, Vanessa. You know that." He said, taking her hand again.

173

"This has nothing to do with my past, but it concerns our future."

She stepped away from him.

"I'm sure you've heard about the witches of Melrose, and my mother being one of them."

Christopher snorted, throwing up his hands.

"Oh come on, Vanessa. You don't really believe that garbage, do you?" He laughed. "My dad also told me some wild and crazy stories. Don't tell me I have to hear it from you too?"

She whirled on him.

"It's not garbage, Christopher! It's the truth! And if we're going to be married, you need to know that I'm one of them. You need to know that and accept it."

She waited pensively for his response.
Christopher's jaw clenched in frustration. If it would make her happy to think she was a witch, then fine. He'd agree to anything to make her happy.

"Alright." He said easily, a grin on his face. "Okay, so you're a witch. I still love you, Vanessa." Vanessa felt the tears fall down her face at his words. She couldn't believe it. He still wanted her.

"You do?" She whispered tremulously. When Christopher saw how much the words meant to her, his heart melted. She truly believed she was a witch.

"Oh baby, come here." He enfolded her within his arms and stroked her hair gently. Vanessa basked in the warmth and love. How could she have ever thought he'd doubt her? Her heart settled as she sighed deeply. She now had the courage to tell him the rest.

"There's more, my love." She said, listening to his steady heartbeat. Christopher continued to stroke her hair. She closed her eyes.

"I'm pregnant."

The gentle stroking abruptly stopped, and she heard his heart shudder inside his chest. He pulled away from her and looked into her eyes.

"W…what did you say?"

"I said I'm pregnant."

Her body was trembling. Her heart thudded rapidly in her chest once again.

All of a sudden, Christopher shouted into the loft, a high yipping sound. Before Vanessa knew what he was doing, he lifted her into his arms. Jumping up and down with loud whoops of joy. She laughed, unable to help herself at his apparent happiness. But she tried to get him to put her down.

"Wait, Christopher!" She laughed, trying to talk to him while he was spinning her. "Christopher, put me

175

down. We still need to talk about this. There's something I have to tell you."

But Christopher was shouting too loud to hear her. Finally, spent and exhausted, he rested her carefully on her feet.

"We have to tell my dad! We have to tell your dad!" Excited, he turned to head down the ladder. Panicked, Vanessa grabbed him.

"Christopher, wait!"

But she didn't have to stop him.

He came to a halt. Frozen to the spot. Poised before the ladder. A strange look coming over his face. Slowly, he turned back towards her. A look of puzzlement and confusion was in his eyes. He frowned at her.

"Wait a second, Vanessa," he said, his frown deepening.

"How could you be pregnant? We haven't made love in almost over a year, until today."

She stared at him. Her heart pounding in her ears.

"That's what I was trying to tell you." She rushed on. "I'm pregnant….. but the baby belongs to my father."

176

CHAPTER TWENTY ONE

Christopher stared at Vanessa for what seemed like an eternity. He stumbled back a few steps, as she tried to reach for him.

"Christopher, please. Let me explain."

He shook his head, trying to clear it of the sudden haze that was enveloping him.

"W…what is this? Some kind of cruel joke?"

His voice stammered in shock and bewilderment. He looked at her. She just stood there staring back at him. An expression of deep despair in her eyes. That scared him even more.

"Answer me, damn it!!" He shouted at her, advancing on her. "Tell me this is some stupid cruel joke you're playing on me!!"

Vanessa stood before him, her shoulders sank, and she lowered her head.

"I'm afraid it's not, Christopher." She said quietly. "It's true. All of it."

She shuddered as a sob tore through her body. Remembering her torment at her father's hands.

"Ever since my mother and aunt Mandy died, he has raped and violated me." Her body shook with violent tremors. "He said to me if I ever told you, if I ever told anyone, he would kill you and them. And I knew he would."

She closed her eyes against the terror of her memories, her father's demonic form, feeding off of her torture and pain. Getting off on abusing and using her.

She cried silently as she told Christopher of the things he used to do to her. The endless nights of torment, the blood and the sacrifices. The demonic power her father wielded over her. She told him of the letters she'd written to him, and how she'd thought he simply didn't want to see her. How her father had lied to keep them apart. She hadn't known until last night, while he'd been raping her. He let it slip how he'd lied to them both.

"I came to you right away, only I knew it was too late. The damage had been done."

Vanessa sobbed as she cradled her flat stomach.

"I knew for sure last week, when I missed my monthly time. And I'm always sick." She looked up then; her face was ravaged with tears, her eyes bleak with sadness.

"I wanted to tell you. I wanted to as soon as I saw you, but I'd missed you so much! Please, Christopher, you have to help me!" She ended on a broken cry. The tears wracking her body.

Christopher looked at her. Her tears called to him. He wanted to wipe them away. To take away her pain. Slowly he walked towards her. Her gaze pleading with him.

"Vanessa." He whispered, his own eyes filling. Softly, he wiped away a lone tear on her cheek.

She never saw it coming.

The sudden crack against her cheek was so powerful, she swung across the hay loft and crashed into the wall with a hard thud. Hitting her head and dazing her.

Christopher stood before her. His fists clenched tightly.

"I don't know what sort of game you're trying to pull. I thought I knew you."

His eyes were laced with contempt and fury.

"I don't know what kind of fool you think I am, telling me some outrageous story like that one! Your father was right." He sneered. Anger vibrating through him. "You are a whore." He turned to leave.

Vanessa looked up at him, the side of her head bleeding from the impact.

His rejection stung. It destroyed her deeper than anything her father could have done to her.
She couldn't bear it.

"Christopher, wait! Don't leave me. Please believe me, I'm telling you the truth!"

She crawled pathetically on her hands and knees and grabbed his leg in desperation. Not caring about herself anymore. All she wanted was him.

But something dark and dangerous glittered in his eyes. Something...inhuman.

Looking down at her, he spat in her face, and kicked her away from him.

"Stay away from me, whore!" He growled at her. A ferocious beast moved within him. "Perhaps my father was right. You are a witch, and you deserve to hang."

With that, he turned and lowered himself down the ladder. Vanessa curled into a ball of pain and cried her heart away. The last piece of her soul tore away from her. It withered and died. She screamed her pain into the night. Christopher could hear her mournful cries as he stalked away.

Leaving behind the only girl he'd ever loved.

CHAPTER TWENTY TWO

Eight Months Later

"She has it Jacob. I know she does. There is nothing left here for us in this godforsaken town! We need the key!"

Carolyn's wicked voice boomed in the silence of the woods. Darkness enveloped them. The trees enclosed them in a cloak of blackness. Jacob watched her with vacant eyes.

The thought of his daughter brought a vile bitter taste in his mouth. He didn't desire her as much as he used to. Her fire seemed to evaporate and diminish. Her huge stomach was round with child. A child he had created.

His body shivered at the thought. It was something he'd fought to keep from the few townspeople that remained. He'd tried in vain to get rid of the child and terminate the pregnancy, but it seemed nothing worked, short of killing her.

It could not be allowed to enter this world.

The fear took hold of him. His master had forbidden it. Vanessa had lost her beauty, her luster. He no longer wanted her.

Perhaps, if he gave her to Carolyn, they could find a way to kill the child. Kill the child and redeem himself in his master's eyes.

He'd escaped death before by promising his master that he would find the key.

Perhaps he still could.

Jacob betrayed none of his thoughts, as he stared at Carolyn.

"Very well then." He said brusquely. "Tomorrow night, when the moon is full, we shall retrieve our key."

Carolyn grinned a slow wicked smile. This time, she would not fail.

***

Vanessa stared out into the night. She was cold. The warm summer air that wafted from her open bedroom window did nothing for her. Nothing did anymore.

She didn't even care that her father hardly touched her anymore. She should've been glad. But she simply did not care.

Each morning she got up and dressed. Her huge stomach was too big for most of her clothes. Her

182

father did not bother to buy her new ones. Vacantly, she stared out at the empty street of the pitiful little town she lived in. More people had moved away. Only half of the families remained. The murders had never been solved, nor, Vanessa knew, would they ever.

She'd recently heard the news of Christopher. He'd just married a woman named Sophia. It was said they had a child together.

Vanessa rose from her bed and went to the window.

She stared up at the stars. They were bright. One was twinkling brighter than the others. So brightly, it looked as if it were blazing red. Vaguely, she remembered a saying her mother used to quote.

'When you see a blazing red star, blazing high in the sky, this is the night to say your
Prayers, for this night you may die.'

Her mother used to say it to get her to say her prayers before she went to bed. But she wondered, looking at the red star, if there was any truth to it. For the first time in eight months, a shiver of fear slithered over her skin.

Death was near. She could feel it.

A cold breeze swept over her face. Like an icy caress. Turning from the window, Vanessa clutched her stomach. The baby kicked viciously, making her gasp.

After all this time, all of these months filled with emptiness, she suddenly realized that she didn't want to die.

Her bedroom door opened, and Jacob stood there. His impassive expression fixed on her.

Vanessa backed into her window.

"Come with me, Vanessa." He said smoothly. "I have something to show you."

He held out his hand. The baby Jumped inside her, restless. Suddenly, Vanessa knew. She knew what would happen if she left with him.

Panicked, she turned to escape out the window, and saw Carolyn's wicked smile staring back at her.

***

Christopher put his son to sleep in his crib. His was now two years old. It still amazed him when he saw him. That one night of passion almost three years ago before he and Vanessa had even met. He hadn't even known Sophia was pregnant, or that the son she'd had was his. He'd asked her to marry him one week after he'd broke it off with Vanessa. That's when she told him that her son was his.

He was angry of course. It seemed as if he was surrounded by lies. But after a while, he'd fallen in love with his little boy. And hadn't thought of Vanessa since. Until now.

Christopher went to the window and stared out at the full moon. He'd discovered So many things about himself, and who he really was, since he left Vanessa.

Things he could no longer deny. And the real reason he could never be with her.

His father was right. He never should've allowed himself to fall in love with her.
They were destined to be enemies.

Vanessa. So sweet. His Vanessa.
But no matter how hard he tried, she was never completely out of his heart.

Suddenly, a feeling of trepidation so strong rose within him. Gasping, he stumbled over to the wall and leaned his back on it. Breathing hard, he looked at his hands. They were trembling.
Changing.

Unbidden, an image of Vanessa rose before him, as if calling him. Terror gripped him as the image wavered, then vanished.

"Vanessa!!"

He shouted, startling his sleeping son. Without thinking, Christopher ran out of the house. He ran faster than he'd ever run before in his life. He had to save her. He had to save his Vanessa.

**

Vanessa opened her eyes. She was outside. Everything was dark. She couldn't see the stars.
The silence was eerie, and it was so cold. Her body shivered violently.
Looking down, she discovered why.
She was completely naked.

Her huge stomach covered her view of everything else. Twisting her head, Vanessa realized she was flat on her back on some sort of board or table. Her arms were stretched out on either side of her, tied down by ropes. Her legs were held down as well. Real terror streaked through her. Her heart thudded wildly in her chest. What was going on? Where was she?

"Hello, my dear." It was her father's voice. He loomed over her.

He was wearing a black hooded cloak; his pale face looked like a vision of death.

A scream lodged in her throat, but it was trapped there. Fear seemed to freeze her insides.

"Do not fear, my beauty." Another voice came from behind her, a woman's voice. "Everything will be just fine."

Vanessa craned her head. The evil beautiful face from her window stared down at her. A memory resurfaced in her mind.

The woman at the funeral. Her mom's nemesis. Carolyn. She too wore a black hooded cloak. That's when she realized it. She was in the woods, and there were five of them in all. She couldn't see them, but she sensed it. Sensed their presence. They all surrounded her. Cloaked in dark garments, preparing for the ritual sacrifice.

And she was it.

Suddenly, her mother's image rose within her.

"Help me!!" Vanessa screamed. She bucked against the ropes; she would not die like this! Carolyn laughed as she watched Vanessa struggle helplessly against her bonds.

"I don't believe she knows how to use her gift, Jacob." She said, mocking her. "Poor, poor innocent one. We shall show you how to use what lies within you."

Carolyn licked her lips and looked at Jacob.

"Let it begin."

CHAPTER TWENTY THREE

Lightening arced thru the dark sky as they began to chant and move.

Carolyn circled her, climbing on top of the table. Vanessa screamed hoarsely, as she felt her fingers move roughly on her skin.

"Stop it!!" She cried in torture. "Please, have mercy!! Don't hurt my baby!!"

The women began to laugh wickedly, as they all climbed on top of her. Kathryn, Amy, Sarah, and Carolyn. Biting her, scratching, squeezing and licking, choking and beating her.

"Kill the child!!" Carolyn shouted. Her eyes were wild and crazed, as she held a black whip. With brute force, she slashed it against Vanessa's body. Across her stomach and face.

"Kill it!!" She took her breasts and squeezed viciously, biting away a piece of her flesh.

 Vanessa was delirious. The pain was unthinkable. Far greater than anything her father had done to her. Carolyn smiled devilishly over her, holding something in her hand. Vanessa's eyes rolled, and she writhed in agony as her skin was branded with a coal iron.

Her baby suffered. Feeling the pain as she felt it. Her body shuddered. Vanessa felt the ripping, and a flood of warm liquid rushed between her legs. She felt her flesh rip open on her arms as they beat her.

Her baby was coming. It was coming and there was nothing she could do about it. She couldn't protect her child; she couldn't even protect herself.

"I don't think you'll be needing this anymore." Carolyn sneered. With a violent tug, she yanked off the gold locket Phoebe had given her and threw it into the darkness.

"Noo!!!" Vanessa screamed helplessly, as she watched the locket disappear.

They shouldn't have done that.

"Mother!!"

The wind howled and raged.
The rains poured onto the earth, into the middle of the woods, where a young woman screamed in fury.

"Yes!!" Jacob cried. Spittle dripped from his mouth. His body swung back and forth in time to the monotone chanting of the witches. He danced and swung around, circling Vanessa's table.

"Do not stop!!" He raged, lifting his hands high above his head. His eyes closed in pleasure, as he began to feel the power. The dark forces screamed in

triumph all around him. The horns protruded and stretched from his head, distorting his face.
His black cloak was ripped away to reveal his naked throbbing body.

The claws in his back stretched longer, and the blood dripped from his deformed demonic body. Vanessa was incoherent, swishing her head from side to side. Unable to control the ferocity inside of her. It was sweet. So potent. With it, she could no longer feel the pain and torment. She was filled with unbelievable power and strength. Her bonds were ripped away from her.

Screaming in rage, she lifted her hands above her. Two silver streaks of lightning shot from the sky straight into her palms. Her body convulsed; her belly moved violently.

The witches were thrown back with the force of the power. Carolyn's eyes widened for the very first time in fear, as she stared.

Vanessa could feel it. The darkness and destruction within her, breaking free. Lightening split a nearby tree. The women jumped out of the way, barely escaping it. Vanessa hollered at her tormentors. Lying bloody with wounds all over her body, she labored. Feeling her baby begin to make its way into the world. She yelled into the sky.

They would pay.

Death and revenge were in her heart, as she prepared the only weapon she knew.

"Hear me now! Let there no longer be one."

There was a rending.

"Separate the life that was before and make it brand new."

The blood on her skin began to sizzle.

"Release that which was before imprisoned, to come forth!"

There was a terrible cracking in the woods.

Vanessa released her gift. Her body jerked as a blinding white light shot from the sky straight into her chest. She cried out. Darkness wrapped around her.

"No!!" Carolyn was hysterical. "Stop her!"

But none of them could reach her.

A deep thunderous roar erupted from the ground. The earth shook and trembled. Carolyn watched in horror, as the ground began to open. Hot scorching flames started to rise from within it. Millions of high-pitched screams rent the air.

"Yes!" Jacob shouted into the fire beginning to surround the woods.

"Come to me my master!! I am waiting for you!!"

Eyes crazed, Carolyn ran to him, her face contorted with rage.

"You stupid fool!!" She ranted at him. Slapping him viciously across the face. "What have you done?!!"

Jacob's blood red eyes narrowed in evil hatred. Cackling hideously, he gripped her neck with his blackened claws, and lifted her above the ground. Squeezing tightly.

"I do not think I have any more use for you, my dear." He rasped loudly over the winds. His snake like tongue slithered out, preparing to open her flesh. Carolyn struggled, terror ripping through her. She was no match for him without the power.

The power Vanessa had now tapped into. She realized too late that Jacob had never intended to help her obtain it. He'd used her for his own gain.

Her body heaved as she began to choke. Her flaming hair flying about in the wind.

"You're forgetting something Jacob!"

She choked out. Straining her words out of her aching throat.

"You did not kill the child. She's already begun to perform the spiritual splitting."

192

Carolyn smiled wickedly. Jacob's eyes widened in fear.

"No! My master has forbidden it!! The child must not live!!!"

He roared inhumanly, flinging her away from him with a powerful thrust. Carolyn crashed through the trees. Pain lanced into her body.

Getting up, she noticed something in the side of her vision. Vanessa's table was surrounded by flames, and a black heavy mist was traveling throughout the woods. She stared, frozen to the spot, as she watched Sarah, Kathryn, and Amy begin to writhe and shake violently, falling to the floor.

Their bodies turning gray.

Screaming in morbid terror, Carolyn turned and ran through the trees. Running from the black mist.

***

A loud crashing sounded, as another figure broke into the clearing.

"Vanessa!!!"

Somewhere within the darkness, she heard his voice.

Christopher stood in the clearing; his eyes wide. Sweat poured from his body. Vanessa lost her concentration at the sight of him. She could see his face through the flames.

193

"No." She whispered, dumbfounded. The incredible renewed pain slicing through her. "It can't be. You helped them? You were here to kill my baby?!!"

Christopher was thrown through the trees by the force of her hatred.

"You did this to me!!!" She screamed out of control.

"Vanessa no!" He shouted over the winds. Tears streaming his face. But he couldn't reach her. No one could. He was too late. He had left her. Abandoned her. And now she was lost.

The blinding rage at seeing Christopher, there with her tormentors, overtook her. It was more than she could withstand. The dam inside of her broke, releasing the key. Lightning bolts streaked from her body, as she lay there, letting the anger and the fury free. It ruled her. It was a beacon in her despair. Fire erupted from her.

"You will all die!!" She shouted through the flames. "You will never live, but you will forever be in a living hell!!!" Vanessa roared as she seemed to explode. Her flesh began to rip in half, as a figure wrenched itself from her body, screaming as it emerged from her, collapsing onto the floor.

She labored, until her baby burst from her, emitting a shrieking cry.

A deep and angry roar shook the earth, at the child's birth. Vanessa cried in torment as she looked at her child for the first and very last time.

"I'm sorry." She whispered. Trembling one final time, as she let the pain go. "I love you."

The tears fell from her, as she closed her eyes forever.

CHAPTER TWENTY FOUR

The figure that had emerged from Vanessa's body was lying on the floor next to her table. It was a young woman. Her hair was streaked with red and black, and her stomach was huge with child. She screamed as she struggled to give birth to the baby moving within her. The flames surrounded them as the baby made its way into the world. Thunder roared. The young woman wept as she looked at the child. It lay very still.

Dead.

Crying in agony, the girl got up. Weeping, she gently touched Vanessa's face.

Taking the squealing baby from the table, she turned and picked up the still born. Carrying both of them, she paused, seeing a small golden object lying on the ground. She picked it up, staring at it. Gently clutching it to her breasts with the babies, she gave one last look at Vanessa's lifeless body, then ran past the flames. Hurrying through the woods.

Her naked body dripped with sweat. She had to escape. She had to get the babies to safety. Running through the darkness, the earth shook, and lightening slashed into the trees. Rain poured down in buckets, making the ground slippery. Suddenly, she felt a presence. No. She had to get away.

In her haste, she stumbled over a rock. The wet
ground making her slip and fall.
Bracing the babies with her body, she rolled. The
impact knocked the children from her grasp.

"No!!!" She screamed as she continued to roll
down a hill, away from the infants.

Her shouts were drowned out by the winds and rain.

A dark shadow loomed over the two babies.
It was Jacob. He looked down on them.

Picking them both up, he took them to his grave pit
where he performed his rituals. Placing the wailing
baby to the side, he picked up the stillborn and placed
it in the shallow grave.

He would please his master, his eyes lit with a red
glow. He would sacrifice these children.

Chanting, he cut his wrist, and placed it in the still
born baby's mouth. He withdrew his bottle and
dripped the contents onto the child's lips. Letting his
blood mix with it. He would resurrect the child, and
then sacrifice them both to his lord.

A huge bolt of lightning slashed through the ground
directly next to him, causing the crying baby to roll
down the hill. Jacob noticed it too late.

"No!!" He lunged. But the child rolled away from
him. Out of sight.

Raging in fury, he turned, and froze.

Christopher stood before him. His body heaving and rasping. His face and chest were bloody, and his shirt was gone. But it was his eyes that Jacob's gaze locked on. Eyes that were blood red like his own.

Jacob snarled. His teeth lengthened, and his claws protruded farther from his back.

"Stay out of this, boy!!" He rasped. "This does not concern you!"

Christopher felt the indomitable power that moved within him. His muscles bulged, and the beast in him growled for blood.

"You killed her." Christopher growled, walking toward him. His face was distorted with rage. "You killed Vanessa, and now you try to kill her child."

His claws lengthened like Jacob's. Horns sprouted from his head. His flesh began to split open, revealing black snakelike skin beneath it.

Jacob jumped to his clawed feet in one smooth motion. Saliva pooling from his open mouth as he hissed at Christopher.

"The child belongs to my master! The same master you serve! Turn away now and let me finish the job!"

198

"I no longer serve your master!" Christopher raged. "I no longer live by his rules, but by my own!!"

"There is no way you can escape it." Jacob cackled viciously. "You may try to deny what you are, but I knew the moment you entered my house. I knew what you hadn't even figured out yet. That you are a demon warlord. And I know what you are destined to do. Now, let me finish it. Let me kill the child, and we can both be victorious in our master's eyes!"

Christopher's body shook. The beast raged within him. He could smell fresh blood.

He wanted to kill the child.

"No!!!" He roared, rearing back his head. Tongue slithering, Christopher slowly advanced on Jacob. A feral look in his demonic eyes.

"You are too late, Jacob." He rasped. His mouth smiling wickedly. "The only death I am about to witness, is yours."

Jacob's eyes widened in sudden realization. Swiveling his head, he looked into the grave pit.

The still born baby was gone.

Christopher leaped into the air and latched himself onto Jacob's neck.

***

Carolyn ran through the woods. Pumping her legs faster and faster. Her heart ramming inside of her chest. She had to escape. Get to the nearest town. If only she could just make it out of the woods. Glancing behind her as she ran, she quickened her pace.

She kept feeling as if something followed. But she could see nothing. Crashing through the trees, she panted. Screaming in fright as something grabbed her hair. It was a tree branch. Wrenching herself free, she ran faster.

She realized with a sudden shock, that she was crying. Low hacking sobs of deep terror. She knew she was being pursued.

"I know who you are!!" She shouted in panic, as she ran through the darkness. The trees seemed to be growing closer together. Like a cage.

"Stay away from me! Stay the fuck away from me!!" Ranting and raving, Carolyn tripped over something, and hurtled headfirst onto the ground, rolling several times.

Panting, she turned to get up.

And stared straight into the eyes of Bethany Simpson.

"No!!!!" Carolyn swung out her fists, but the image was gone. Leaping up, she tried to run, but came face to face with Roselyn Jackson. Her Vacant eyes staring at her. Her flesh bleeding and hanging in torn pieces from how she'd been sliced repeatedly.

Carolyn could hear the screams now. The screams of the damned, and the tormented.

"Stop it!!" She covered her ears with her hands and spun in a circle. Trying to escape the visions before her.

Falling to her knees, she cried out. Her eyes were crazed and filled with terror. Through the torment, she felt something. A sinister presence.

Turning around, it was the last thing she ever saw.

Small hands ripped her flesh and tore her body. Eating her bones as she was dragged beneath the earth.

Her screams now joined those of the damned.

***

Jacob stood over Christopher's limp beaten body. Heaving. Blood gushing from the wounds on his head and neck.

"It is over for you, boy!!" Jacob rasped. His claws lengthening to even greater in size.

"Did you really think that you could defeat me?" He laughed wickedly. "I am Jacob Dickens! And I am perfect!!" He laughed as he prepared to rip through his body.

Christopher watched him through half open eyes, blood pouring from his flesh. He had changed back into his human form, and he was ready to die.

Suddenly, Jacob turned around at something behind him. His body going still.

"No." He said, his voice shaking. "No, it can't be!! You're dead! You're not alive!!"

Jacob screamed in terror.

He turned back towards Christopher, surprise and shock swam through his blood red eyes.

Christopher watched as Jacob sank to his knees. His face shone with indescribable pain and torment.

"You were right." He rasped out. "It's too late. Too late for us all."

He looked on, his eyes widening with fright, as Jacob's eyeballs fell from his face. His skull split open, and a small hand emerged from his chest. Gripping his still beating heart.

Christopher stared as the thing ate Jacob's organ, pausing to look up at him.

It was the last thing he remembered, as darkness closed over him.

The red glowing eyes. The promise of death to come.

***

Stillness reined throughout the town of Melrose. Dawn never came.

No one ever left their beds or walked the streets again. It was known wide and far that it was the town of the dead. Citizens from surrounding areas spoke in hushed whispers about a curse. The People of Melrose were never heard from again. No one dared venture close enough to investigate further.

The case was closed.

The entire tragedy covered up by state officials. No one was allowed to speak of it again.

Christopher McMann sat in his ranch home, relaxing in a chair. Wondering how and why he'd escaped. His sad listless eyes stared out of the window.
Always watching. Always waiting. For he knew the terror was not over.

He knew it was only a matter of time.

***

Miles away, a baby's angry cry could be heard.
As a mother gently cradled the child to her breast, the baby's eyes shimmered with a red glow.

Stay tuned for Blood of my Blood Book 2: The Recognition – Samantha and Sunflower

Coming soon!

Turn the page for an exclusive preview of Book 2

PROLOGUE

1987

The woman panted heavily as her muscles strained and flexed. Her voice was sore from screaming. Sweat poured down her body, completely soaking her hospital gown.

"Come on, I need you to breathe. Concentrate on your breathing."

The doctor gripped the woman's legs and encouraged her, all the while watching the small baby's progress, as it began to make its entrance.

"Please!!" The woman screamed as another contraction shook through her body.

Her husband grabbed her hand. A worried frown puckered his brow. Fear lanced through him. There seemed to be some complications with the birth. His wife had been laboring for two days now. If the baby didn't make its entrance soon, she would have to go into surgery.

The woman shouted and threw her head back. Her short brown hair was pasted to her head. Her face was a mask of torture, grimacing with pain.

"Okay, push, push, push!" The doctor shouted, making eye contact with the nurses who were scrambling to give assistance.

"No! I can't! I just can't do it anymore!" The woman wept, swishing her head back and forth.

"Yes you can, baby. I'm right here." Her husband cupped her face and smiled reassuringly.
"I know you can do it. Hold on to me, baby."

She wept harder and closed her eyes. With a deep low grunt, her body concentrated on pushing the small burden into the world.

She screamed in triumph, as the child made way, coming headfirst with a whoosh, into the doctor's hands.

***

The nurse cleaned the baby up. Washing it and checking to make sure all was well.
The mother lay peacefully sleeping in the labor recovery room.

Her husband had gone to make happy phone calls. The nurse placed the small baby in the incubator and rolled it out of the room.

The hospital was very quiet at this time of morning. It was only three am, and shifts wouldn't change for another three hours. Smiling in greeting at the women at the front desk, the nurse slowly rolled the incubator down the hall.

The nursery room was the last door on the right. She entered, smiling at another nurse sitting down in a rocking chair, cradling a baby.

The woman in the rocker glanced up as she came in. Their smiles both widened in their faces.

Going over to an empty incubator, the nurse rolled the newborn child next to it, and lifted the baby into her arms.

"Beautiful Little baby." She cooed. The female infant eyes stared back at her, curiously.
The woman sitting in the rocker, cradling another child, got up and walked over to her.

"She is beautiful." She agreed.

Slowly, both women placed the babies in two incubators directly next to each other. The first nurse smiled down at the infant the other woman had been rocking to sleep.

"I think she'll like this one, Tammy." She said. "This family fits the description perfectly."

"I agree, Debbie." Tammy replied. "The waiting is over. After years of switching from family to family, I believe we've finally found the perfect bait." Debbie grinned in response. A peculiar glint in her eyes.

"This family will bring her to us." She whispered softly.

Debbie withdrew the name plate from the incubator of the baby she rolled into the room. Smiling, she placed it in the one directly next to it and slid a new plate inside of the original.

Tammy grinned down at the baby she'd been rocking, and the new name plate directly over its head. As she smiled, her teeth revealed sharp points, and a tongue as long as a snake.

Her nails curled like claws, and her eyes were blood red.

Debbie stood next to her, looking at the child as well. Her eyes flaming, her tongue was slithering.

"It is done, my queen." She rasped, her evil smile widening. "We have placed you with another family. And this time, we have not failed you."

Tammy cackled in glee.

"It is only a matter of time."

The baby Tammy had been rocking opened its eyes. The raging fires of hell swam within them, as they shimmered with a bright red glow.

Yes. It was only a matter of time.

About The Author

Born and raised in the Bronx, NY. Andrea Johnson was writing from the age of ten. She wrote and produced the first stage play in her junior high school, created paranormal short stories for her High School newspaper, and formed the youth group: G.G.S (God's Given Saints) at the age of twelve.

She is the CEO and President of a small marketing firm, co-owner of an insurance agency, and founder of Andrea Johnson Books Publishing. As well as the host of the electrifying web series: Bedtime Mysteries. She directs and manages fund raising campaigns and community organizations for Christian development and female empowerment.

Her first book, Blood of my Blood was released in 2009 and created inspiration to young new writers. Her stories have a reputation for the wild and unusual, and have been an entertainment for many years. Her motto is: make each day count, and live each day as if it were your last.

Andrea lives in Dallas, TX with her family, her German Shepherd, Prince, and beautiful black cat Rubia.

Visit Andrea's website to learn more about her upcoming books!

www.AndreaJohnsonBooks.com